RETURN TO BLACKCREEK

A Blackcreek Anthology

By Riley Hart

Dedication

This book is dedicated to my readers. Thank you for your support. I couldn't do this without you. I'm thankful for each and every one of you, each and every day. I hope you enjoy your return to Blackcreek as much as I did.

BRADEN
&
WES

-1-
Early December

B RADEN HAD A plan. It was something he'd had brewing for quite some time. For a while he tried to talk himself out of it. It would complicate things. He had to make sure everyone was one hundred percent on board, but the more he tried to make himself change his mind, the more he realized he didn't want to. This was an ache inside him that wouldn't go away. A fire that burned deep in his gut, blazing hotter with each passing day.

Finally, he'd decided to try and figure out how to make it work, which definitely wasn't easy. Especially since he was keeping it from Wesley.

He hated doing that, but when it came to his guy, Braden knew what was best. And in this situation, it was best that Braden go to Wes with all the answers prepared, with everything figured out, and then show him just how incredibly fucking amazing it would all be.

Because it would be.

Wesley would think so as well. He just worried so goddamned much sometimes. It was Braden's job to take the worry away from him.

And fuck his brains out. Braden really loved that he was the one who got to do that every night.

Braden shifted on the couch as he heard a sound behind him.

"She's ready for us," Wes said from the hallway. Braden pushed to his feet and walked to meet him.

"You have dried paint on your forehead." Braden pressed his lips next to the spot of green paint. "You're so messy. Wanna get

3

messy with me later tonight? You can fuck me and then I'll paint you with my co—"

"Daddy! Daddy Braden, I'm ready! Huuurrrry!" Jessie called from her room, the sound cooling Braden's hormones but warming his heart. Jesus, he'd become such a sappy, emotional man since he found his family.

He wouldn't change a second of it, though.

"We're being summoned. We better go before she kicks our asses," Braden said as Wes threaded their fingers together. Jessie would definitely kick their asses, too. He wasn't exaggerating. She was only seven, but tough and used to getting her way. They spoiled her. Wes told him that all the time, but Braden didn't see a problem with it. She was a good kid and they loved her. That's all that mattered.

The two of them made their way into their girl's room as she lay in her bed, her blond curls longer than they had been a few years ago when Braden came into their lives. A lot had happened in that time. They were married and settled happily in their home. They'd adopted Jess. She started calling Wes "Daddy" not long after, and then one day Braden had come home from work and Wes told him Jessie asked if she could call Braden some form of dad as well.

It was one of the best days of his life. Coming home to his husband and Jessie was way better than partying and fucking random people, even if half the time he acted like a big kid himself. Life was more fun that way.

"You ready for bed, Squirt?" Braden plopped down on the bed beside her, making the whole thing shake.

"Yes, but you guys are slooooow."

"Not me, it was that guy." Braden pointed at Wes who rolled his eyes at them.

"Um, who's the one who came to get you? Jess and I were ready. You're the one who had your butt on the couch, complete-ly lost in thought." Wes scratched at the dark scruff on his face that Braden fucking loved so much. It felt good against his skin.

He couldn't wait to feel it rubbing against him tonight.

"He's right. You've been weird." Jessie poked his side. Perceptive little girl. He *did* have a lot on his mind. The more time passed, the more he had filling his head, and now he was on countdown mode to the point when he'd be able to let the cat out of the bag.

"Braden!" Jessie said when he didn't reply to her.

"*You're* weird." Braden returned her poke from earlier, trying not to seem so distracted.

"Am not."

"Are too."

"Am not."

"Excuse me, kids," Wes interrupted them with a grin on his face. "Can we start our bedtime reading now? Jess has school in the morning."

"Ugh, always so boring." Braden winked at him. "What are you reading us—ugh," he grunted when Jock, their chocolate lab, jumped on the bed. He'd taken the dog's spot beside Jess. Her second dog, Prince Eric, was curled up on the dog bed on the floor. They both slept with her, but Jock had the reserved spot beside her. He'd claimed Jess even more quickly than Braden had claimed his family back when they first met.

Braden sat up and got out of the dog's way before Wes sat down beside him. "She wants to start Harry Potter."

They made it a habit to read Jessie a chapter out of a book each night. She loved fantasy. They'd finished a book about a girl and a pegasus last night, and now it was time for a new one. "Ooh, Harry. I've seen the movies but haven't read the books. You start. I'll read next time," Braden told him.

He and Jessie paid rapt attention as Wes read to them, his deep, smooth, steady voice working its way inside Braden the way it always did. That was Wesley—their steady calm. Braden was the one who always wanted to shake things up.

After they finished reading, Braden stepped back and watched as Wes bent and kissed Jessie's forehead, telling her goodnight.

She tightened her little hands around his neck, clinging to him, Wes doing the same to her. Wes didn't know how strong his influence was on people. That little girl thought the world of him, the same way Braden did. She'd changed him. She changed both of them and Braden was thankful for them every day.

When Wes stepped back it was Braden's turn. He ruffled her hair, making her giggle before leaning forward, mouth close to her ear. "Remember what we talked about for this weekend?" he whispered.

She nodded and when Braden pulled back, she winked at him. She was so much older than her years in some ways. "Night, Squirt."

"Night, Daddy Braden," she replied before curling up on her side. Braden and Wes slipped out of the room, turning out the light and closing the door as they left.

Wes backed him up toward their bedroom, closing Braden in against the wall. His firm, strong body molded against Braden's as he slipped a hand under Braden's shirt to rest on his side. He knew if he looked, Wes would have paint under his fingernails.

"I want you," Wes said against his ear.

Just having Wes so close to him made his dick start to harden, and his body heat shoot up. Yes, they could definitely fuck, but—

"We can do that. But we should probably pack first." His pulse kicked up. Jesus, he was nervous. He couldn't believe he was fucking nervous. Braden didn't work that way.

Wes's dark brows pulled together. "Pack?"

"Yes. I'm the world's best husband. I planned a weekend away for us. I made sure we were both off work. Lydia's going to pick Jess up after school. Noah and Coop are taking the dogs. Gavin and Mason offered to water the plants, but I told them we don't have any, and said they could watch the house instead, even though we don't really need the house watched. Mason offered us the use of one of his family's cabins, which was a better idea. Smart guy, that bartender. Anyway, that's where we're headed— to a cabin for the weekend."

Wes chuckled, curling his hand in Braden's shirt. "You've been busy."

"I have been. That's because I'm...come on...fill in the blank."

He grinned and Wes leaned forward, covering Braden's mouth with his. His tongue probed Braden's lips and he immediately opened up to let his man inside. He knew everything about Wes—how he kissed, how he moved, how every part of him tasted, and he couldn't get enough. He never would.

Wes's grip on his hip tightened and he thrust against Braden, who moaned into Wes's mouth. Oh yeah, he couldn't wait to get the man alone for the weekend. Wes's lips left his mouth, trailing down his neck. "Best. Husband. Ever," he said between kisses, filling in the blank as Braden had suggested. "What'd I do to deserve a surprise trip?" he asked, still kissing and licking at Braden's skin.

"You just have to be you. That's it. I always want to be with you."

He just hoped Wes still felt the same way about him after their weekend.

-2-

JESSIE HAD BEEN right. Braden was definitely acting weird. He'd had little bursts of strange behavior off and on for the past few months. Nothing major, and it wasn't as though Wes was really worried. They were okay, they were fucking happy and he knew they always would be, but he also knew Braden. His husband had something on his mind and even though Wes was curious as hell, he'd let it play out, waiting for Braden to clue him in. He was used to Braden's big ideas now.

Maybe some of it was also a self-preservation thing. As much as he loved Braden and even though Wes *was* getting better about things, he had to admit Braden's starry eyes sometimes scared him. He would always be the worrier in the relationship and Braden would always be the happy optimist. That's just who they were. Maybe that's why they worked so well—they balanced each other out.

Snow covered the ground, white all along the trees and mountains as they made their way down the winding road and out of town. Braden was behind the wheel of his truck, Wes in the passenger seat, watching him. "You're being quiet. You're never quiet."

Braden risked a quick glance at him but then focused on the road again. Wes continued to watch him. He knew the exact color of Braden's green eyes. Watched his narrow jawline work. Paid attention to Braden's tongue lick the lips he'd had wrapped around Wes's cock last night. And then he smiled, the familiar, bright, happy fucking smile that lit up the whole goddamned world. Wes loved that smile.

"Are you saying I have a big mouth?"

"Yes."

"Hey! You don't mind my mouth when it's on your dick. Maybe I'll have to keep it to myself from now on."

Okay, so he wanted to play coy. And stall. Wes could see it, and he decided to let him. Again, partially for Braden and partly for himself. "No keeping that sexy, fucking thing to yourself. I didn't say I mind your mouth. I just said you use it a lot. I happen to like how you use it." One of his favorite things in the world was listening to Braden talk. He saw the world so different-ly than anyone Wes had ever known. It would be a crime to rob the world of Braden's words.

"I'll be sure to use it a lot this weekend then. Mason said the cabin is stocked with food. We won't have to leave the whole weekend. We'll get it warm in there and then I think we need to have a no-clothes rule. We do everything naked. First we'll fuck, and then you can paint. We'll fuck again and then we'll eat, shower, fuck, talk, fuck, and then maybe we'll fuck some more. We're both going to have sore asses by the time we leave." He glanced Wes's way and winked at him again. That sounded like the perfect weekend to Wes.

"Promise?" he asked, reaching over to lay a hand on Braden's thigh.

"Oh yeah, baby. You know it. We're going to have each other in every way possible this weekend."

But there was more to this and Wes knew it.

A few years ago, he would have lost his mind with worry, but now? Now, he trusted Braden. That didn't mean that whenever he figured out what Braden wanted to talk to him about, he wouldn't freak the fuck out. There were no guarantees on that, but he'd cross that bridge when he came to it.

With his hand still on Braden's leg, Wes closed his eyes. His lips stretched into a smile when he felt Braden's warm, strong hand over his, and then from there...nothing...

"Wesley, wake up. We're here."

It was funny how much he used to hate going by his full name. If anyone else tried to call him Wesley, they wouldn't get an answer. Not Braden, though. He'd tried to tell Braden not to use the name but that hadn't lasted long. Hell, if he were being honest, he'd admit he probably liked it from the start. Despite his protests, he might have always wanted to be someone different to Braden.

"Open your eyes, Wesley. I see you smiling, so stop thinking about me and go inside and get naked with me instead. We get to have sex in a house without a kid in it. We need to take advantage."

That got Wes's eyes open for more reasons than one. There was the obvious—the sex. He couldn't get enough of Braden. But then there was the other part of it. Even though they'd been together for a few years now, things like that still took him by surprise sometimes. This man could be anywhere in the world doing anything he wanted, yet he chose to marry Wes. Chose to take Jessie as his kid. Chose being a father and not being able to fuck when and wherever he wanted. Not getting to walk around the house naked the way he said he wanted to do this weekend. It made Wes open his mouth and say, "Thank you."

"For being sexy?" Braden cocked a dark brow at him.

"That's one reason."

"For the weekend, then? Or because I want to get naked with you so badly? I think I'm going to suck your dick for hours. You can sit on the couch and watch TV, or find a chair and paint, and I'll just be on my knees with your dick in my mouth. You know how much I love sucking your cock."

Blood rushed to Wes's prick at that. Yes, he did know how much Braden loved sucking him off. He sure as hell knew how much he loved being on the receiving end. "All of the above?" Wes's words sounded like a question even to his own ears, but he didn't want it to sound like a question because he was sure. "For everything—this weekend, and for choosing us."

"Always." Braden ran a hand through Wes's dark hair. "You're being awfully sentimental."

He was. Maybe because he felt Braden being on edge lately. He just knew he always wanted Braden to know how lucky he felt because of the life they lived together. He knew Braden was happy. They all were. He didn't have any real doubts about their relationship or anything like that. He loved the man sitting next to him and knew Braden loved him...but he also knew Braden had options. He didn't have to tie himself down to Wes and Jessie but he had, and he made their lives fucking perfect. He made Wes really live instead of just getting by. "That's because I love you."

"I love you, too. Can we go inside and get naked now? I'm really fucking dying to spend the weekend naked with you."

"Yeah," Wes smiled. "We can go get naked now." He couldn't wait.

-3-

THEY GRABBED THEIR bags and Braden led Wes up the snow-covered wood porch. It was a small cabin, but that's all they needed. He fished the key Mason had given him from his pocket, unlocked the door, and they stepped into the living room.

Off to the left was a fireplace with a stack of wood beside it. The room had a deep brown couch, a coffee table, and a TV on the wall directly in front of him. There was an entrance to the hallway on the same wall as the TV. He knew there was only one room down that hall with a pretty fucking incredible shower from what Mason had said. On the other side of the living room was a small dining room table and the kitchen.

"It's perfect," Wes said from behind him.

"Yeah, yeah it is. We'll do a fire later. Close the door. I'm going to hit the heat so we can get naked now."

He heard the door close behind him as he moved toward the thermostat on the wall.

There was a loud rumble and then the heater kicked to life. "Come on, Wesley. I want to take a shower with you." Sure, he was changing up the schedule from what he'd said in the truck, but the shower would be worth it.

His dick was already hard. He could tell from the low growl behind him that Wes was as hard and turned on as he was. It was so fucking amazing to know someone so well—inside and out, every part of him, the way he did his husband.

They walked to the end of the hallway and opened the door to the bedroom. The room was as big as the living room, kitchen and dining room combined.

Directly across from the door was a king-sized bed. There was a sliding glass door that lead to a deck with a hot tub that they wouldn't be able to use because of the weather. He'd have to remember to ask Mason if they could come back this summer.

When Braden saw the bathroom he said, "This way," and then walked over.

It was huge. Mason hadn't been lying about the shower. It was probably the size of three of their showers at home, with a bench inside and dual showerheads on adjacent walls. The walls were black and gray granite, the other two glass. In the corner of the room was a Jacuzzi they could definitely put to good use as well.

"Holy shit," Wes said from behind him and Braden heard the bag fall from his hand and hit the floor.

Braden turned, grabbed Wes's sleeve and pulled his husband close. "Naked. All weekend, remember?" With quick hands he pushed Wes's jacket off his shoulders, and then shrugged out of his own. They were both frantic as they pulled their shirts over their heads and hurried out of their jeans.

Wes's long, thick cock sprung free, bouncing against his belly. His dick had been in Braden's hands, mouth, and ass too many times to count over the years. He had every inch of Wes memorized and yet, fire still shot through him every time he saw the man's gorgeous, naked body. "Nice view," Braden grinned at him.

Wes's stare grew more intense, as though he was searching deep inside of Braden for something. "You said that to me the first time we had sex at the house. On Thanksgiving. You remember that?"

"I do. I remember everything."

"I do, too." And then Wes's mouth crashed down on his. They were a frenzied tangle of hands rubbing and touching each other, the whole time keeping their mouths fused together. He knew everything about this man—his taste, what he liked and how he felt. They had an active sex life, liked to switch things up so there was no monotony, but at the same time everything about Wes and what they had was familiar. He never thought he would want something comfortable like that but he fucking loved it.

"Come on. And grab the lube." As soon as Wes grabbed it, Braden tugged him to the oversized shower. His husband came easily. As Braden turned the faucet he felt Wes's lips on his back, right over his tattoo.

"Out of the ashes," he whispered referring to Braden's phoenix tattoo. "Like being reborn. That's what you did for me."

Jesus they were so fucking mushy right now. He couldn't find it in himself to care. "Stop or you're gonna make me blush."

Wes let out a loud laugh behind him. "Yeah right. Your head's too big for that."

See? Wes knew Braden just as well as Braden knew Wes. "Come on, Wesley." As soon as he got the temperature right, they stepped into the shower. Their lips immediately found each other's again as they kissed, licked, and bit at each other's mouths. Wes's hard body rubbed against him, their cocks brushing as they made out under the warm spray.

It wasn't enough. He'd had the man too many times to count but it was suddenly like their first time. Like he had to grab on and take advantage of doing nasty, dirty, sexy things to Wes because the man might change his mind. He knew Wes wouldn't. Not really. They were solid, but sometimes that need reared up inside him to stake his claim, to fuck Wes like he wasn't lucky enough to do it every day if he wanted.

Braden shoved Wes against the wall. "Oh fuck," Wes grunted out as soon as his body made contact. They were out from under the spray now and Braden immediately went down.

"You know how much I love being on my knees for you. I could suck your dick all day, and we both know I'm fucking good at it." Braden looked up at Wes, into those hazel, contemplative eyes that always held so much.

"Always talkin'."

"You like it."

"I still do. Now put my dick in your mouth. We can talk later."

Braden almost laughed. He'd said something similar to Wes years ago, *"I'm kidding. I have a big mouth. Put your dick in it so I stop talking."* He had less of a problem of *open mouth, insert foot,* now than he had back then.

Right now, he didn't want to laugh. He wanted to blow his husband. Braden went for it, took Wes deep, all the way to the fucking root.

"Jesus Christ, that mouth of yours. I love it so much." Wes's hand went to Braden's head, guiding him, pushing him back down on his cock every time Braden slid off. Wes's hips flexed as he fucked Braden's mouth. Each time his prick hit the back of his throat, Braden swallowed.

Wes was incredibly hard, so fucking hard and wet from the water and Braden's mouth. He traced the veins in Wes's erection with his tongue. Pulled off and licked the slit, sucked his crown, and then went down toward his heavy balls. "You're ready to bust at any second," he said before sucking the tight sac into his mouth. Wes's rough pubic hair rubbed his face which just made Braden take him deeper, shove his face into Wes's crotch to mark himself with red skin from the friction.

"Fuck, that feels so good. I'll never get tired of that mouth of yours, baby. Take my cock again."

Braden did as Wes said, sucking the long, swollen rod into his mouth. His eyes watered he took Wes so deep, but he didn't care. He wanted it all. Wanted to eat his come too, but didn't want Wes to orgasm before he fucked him.

"That's enough. Stop. Fuck, you gotta stop or I'm going to come," Wes said breathlessly, and then pulled Braden to his feet. "We're good. You can fuck me. I knew I'd want your dick in my ass the second we got here."

Braden leaned in, pressed a quick kiss to Wes's lips. "Still can't get enough of me, huh?"

"Nope. Never."

That was exactly what Braden wanted to hear.

"**L**ET ME GET the lube," Braden said, kissing his ear. He loved the sound of Braden's voice, loved hearing him talk all the time, but especially when it was full of lust and desire.

For him. Always for him.

Wes grabbed the lube from the seat in the shower. "Hurry up and take me, Braden. Want you so fucking much." He heard the lust from Braden's voice mirrored in his own. He wanted Braden in every way right now. Wanted rough and primal Braden to fuck him. Wanted his husband to make love to him. They had time for everything, he reminded himself, even though he knew they were here for something serious, too.

"Yes, sir!" Braden teased and then with eager hands turned Wes so his chest was against the wall. "Ass out, baby."

His front molded to Wes's back. Jesus, he loved the feel of this man behind him. Loved his hard body, his cock, the feel of his hair and his mouth and his arms around him. "I'm waiting," he said, wiggling his ass against Braden's engorged cock.

"Mmm…an impatient little bottom today, aren't we?"

Wes spread his legs, giving Braden easier access, and then he felt a cold, slick finger at his hole. A tremor ran down his spine. "Get something inside me, Braden." As soon as Braden's name left his lips, his husband pushed a finger in, then another, fucking him with the lubed digits.

In, out, in out, Braden didn't tease him long, just stretched his hole, getting him ready for what they really wanted.

Suddenly, his body was empty, but not for very long. Braden's slick erection breached him, pushed past the ring of muscle and then slammed home. "Oh fuck." There was a slight burn, then stretching, and the incredible fucking feeling of being filled by this man.

Braden kept him away from the water, probably to avoid washing the lube away. He pulled out and then thrust forward again. Wes called out, fisted his hands against the wall. Even his goddamned toes curled.

Braden's arms encircled him from behind, wrapped around his waist, then up so that he held onto Wes's shoulders.

"More," Wes groaned out, and Braden gave it to him. He jackhammered into Wes, hard. Each time he pulled almost all the way out, Wes's body ached to be filled again. Then he'd slam in and Wes would feel complete again.

"You feel so fucking good, Wesley. There's nothing like lovin' you." And then Braden's teeth bit into the muscle in Wes's neck. A moan ripped from Wes's lips.

He shoved his hips back, meeting each of Braden's passionate thrusts. Their bodies slapped together. The shower was starting to turn cold, but it didn't matter, nothing did except his husband taking him.

Braden shoved inside Wes, fucking him fast and hard. Each time Braden pumped inside him, Wes's body tensed in the best way.

When one of Braden's hands slid down his body and wrapped around Wes's aching erection, he almost lost it right there.

"Gimme your mouth, Wesley. Want my tongue in it." Braden nipped at his ear and then Wes turned. It was an awkward angle, Braden fucking him from behind. One arm holding onto him, the other jacking him off as Wes turned his head to kiss him but they made it work. Braden's tongue swept his mouth. His lips moved hungrily with Wes's.

The hold on his dick got tighter, each stroke faster as Braden still pounded into him from behind.

"This is perfect. Our lives are perfect," slipped past Wes's lips and Braden stumbled slightly, lost his rhythm as though what

Wes just said had been the wrong thing somehow. He gained it right back though, shoving into Wes in the most delicious way.

"My balls are aching here. If you don't come soon I'm going to ruin this before you get off," Braden said in his ear.

Wes wrapped a hand around Braden's, jacking himself off with his husband, then let his hand drift down to his own sac, playing with it. Braden's balls slapped against him; he pulled almost all the way out and then slammed forward again, hitting the exact spot Wes needed him to. His balls drew tighter, little blasts detonating inside him before the main event. He let go, white jets of come exploding from his slit, the sticky fluid making Braden's hand glide even more easily up and down his cock.

"Oh fuck," Braden gritted out behind him, and then Wes felt him tense, felt him shove deeper as he filled Wes with spurt after spurt of come.

Wes's knees went weak, but Braden held him up. Or maybe they were holding each other up, his body squeezed between Braden's and the shower wall. Neither of them spoke, just breathed heavily as Braden held him from behind, arms still wrapped tightly around him.

It felt like an eternity before Wes made himself ask, "Why are we here, Braden?"

Braden nuzzled into Wes's neck, and Wes closed his eyes, savoring the feeling of this man he loved so fucking much. "I wanna have a baby with you," he said softly. Wes felt...he didn't know what he felt. His gut twisted, though he couldn't say why. Shock, maybe? His heart sped up and his brain ran with a million questions.

When he couldn't figure out how to reply, he said, "I don't think we have all the right equipment for that." He wasn't completely surprised by what Braden said, though. He knew it would come up eventually, probably knew it would come up this very weekend. That was Braden. Jesus, he was so fucking good with Jess. The best dad a kid could want. Of course he would want another baby. The question was, did Wes? It was much easier to think about Braden.

"Funny guy. I know you're freaking out in that head of yours." He kissed Wes's temple. "But don't. And don't reply yet either. I don't want you to answer me until the weekend is over, and I promise you, I'll understand either way. I'm not going anywhere, Wesley, no matter what. I can promise you that. You and Jess are mine...but I need you to know, I want this, too. I love you so fucking much, and I want to grow our family together."

Wes let out a deep breath, turned and then wrapped his arms around Braden. It was him who buried his face in Braden's neck this time. Still, his mind went a million miles an hour and no matter how much he tried to stop it, he couldn't.

Another kid.

A baby.

It was a big step.

"I love you too," he told Braden, who leaned back and winked at him.

"I know. How could you not?" He nodded toward the shower door. "Come on. Let's get out of here before my dick freezes off."

"We wouldn't want that." Wes grinned, and Braden laughed. Still, his mind was back on what Braden had said...that he wanted a baby. And he knew Braden was still thinking about it as well.

-5-

"SO ARE WE keeping up with this naked thing?" Wes asked him after they got out of the shower and dried off. Some of the weight in Braden's chest let up. Wes had grown so much since they'd fallen in love. He'd changed. Yes, sometimes he still worried too much or thought about things too much. He had trouble thinking about the good that could happen rather than the bad, but that's just who he was. The fact that he made a joke just now showed how far he'd come.

"I'd like your cock and ass on display for me all weekend, but it hasn't quite warmed up yet. Clothes for a little while, but next time we strip each other out of them, we lose them for good."

Wes gave him a simple nod. They dressed in sweats, sweat-shirts and socks before making their way out of the bathroom.

"I could live in there," Wes said.

"No shit. Except I'm a little hungry. I'm thinking eating in the kitchen is a better idea."

Before their weekend, Braden had given Mason some cash so he could make sure the house was stocked with food. He didn't want to have to leave for anything before it was time.

They made coffee, grilled cheese sandwiches and tomato soup together. They'd gotten a little better at cooking over the years and it was something they often did together. Jess would help and they'd make it a big family thing, which she really enjoyed.

"It's quiet without her." Braden set his plate on the table, just before Wes did the same.

"I know. On the one hand it's nice to get away and have you to myself, but I miss her, too."

Braden felt the exact same way. And if they were going to have a baby, time for just the two of them would be harder to come by.

Braden watched Wes as he took a drink of his coffee, and then set the cup down. "Talk to me. I know you. You have this whole thing figured out, so break it down for me. Even the cost alone is something we have to consider. It's outrageously expensive to—"

"Not if you have a donor already, and not if they're family." Wes's eyes widened. Braden took a deep breath and let it all out. "I talked to Lizzy and her husband, and they would both love to do this for us. She'll carry the baby. We'll use her egg, your swimmers, and that way the baby will carry both of our DNA." That didn't mean it wouldn't still be pricey, but this made it much more manageable.

Wes frowned, which Braden had expected. "Is that weird? To have your sister carry our baby? And her husband is okay with that? Nine months is a long time. This is a big deal."

Braden rolled his eyes. "First of all, it's not weird. People do it all the time. My sisters both loved being pregnant. We have a fucking army at our house. Lizzy is excited to make that army bigger for us. To give us a baby. She knows it's a big deal, as do I. This wasn't a decision that was made in the spur of the moment, Wesley. We've been talking about it for months. She's gone to the doctor, and had conversations with her husband. The four of us will sit down and talk before we move forward with anything. You can ask whatever questions you want and if you'd rather we ask Lydia we can—"

"What? No. I can't believe you just suggested that. You know I love your family like they're my own. It's not that I have a problem with it being your sister. I just…this isn't something to take lightly. And will it be awkward? With it being your sister's egg that means it's her baby. But if we do this, I'd want the child to be part of both of us, and that's really the only way to make that happen." Wes shook his head. "Jesus, are we really talking about this? Are we really thinking of having a baby?"

Braden's heart warmed. He knew a part of Wes really wanted this. He believed a part of Wes wanted it before Braden brought it up to him, but he also knew Wes's first instinct was fear. "We are." A fucking baby. Sometimes he couldn't believe this was his life.

"Even if Lizzy carries the baby, it's still not cheap. And we have jobs to consider—"

"I'll fucking quit if I have to," Braden said. He'd miss fighting fires like crazy but he'd do it. He'd do anything for their family. "I can always go back to work when the baby's a couple of years old."

"No. Fuck that. You'd lose your mind if you stopped working. We both know that. You love what you do too much."

"I'd love our baby more." And he would. A job was just that, a fucking job.

"I know," Wes said, sincerity in his voice. He looked at Braden like Braden could do no wrong. Like the sun rose and set on him. Braden was a confident man. He always had been. He played it up as well, joking and teasing about knowing how good he was at this or that, but the way Wes looked at him? It made him feel like the most important man in the world. Nothing else mattered except for the way Wes and Jessie saw him. The way his family loved him. As long as they loved him, as long as Wes continued to look at him like he did now, that was all he needed. Who cared what anyone else thought? He was the luckiest man on earth.

"We could do this, Wesley. We have so much love to give. We can do this and I promise you, everything will be okay. I promise you'll be the best god damned dad in the world to our baby, the same way you are to Jess."

Wes gave him a small, sad, smile and nodded. "Thank you."

There were still a million questions and concerns in his eyes. He needed to sort through them and Braden would give him the space to do so. "Why don't we eat and then you can bring your painting supplies in. Get a little painting done and I'll hang out, watch some TV or something for a while."

"Okay." Wes stood up, moved his chair and food closer to Braden and sat down again. They both ate one-handed, their other hands latched together the whole time.

-6-

WES SET UP in the bedroom. The floor was hardwood, and he placed plastic down so he didn't risk getting paint on it. He'd tried to tell Braden he wouldn't need his supplies this weekend, but of course, Braden had known better than that. He knew it would help Wes clear his head. Painting always did that, as did the man pretending to watch television in the living room to give Wes the space he needed.

He'd taken a blank canvas with him, leaving his partially finished painting at home. Hell, he didn't even know what he wanted to create, but the *what* of it didn't much matter right now. He just needed to do…something.

He picked up a pencil and put it to the canvas, ready to sketch…but nothing came.

Wes dipped the paintbrush in blue, then placed it to the canvas, so close it almost touched, yet he didn't transfer the color to the white, blank space.

"Fuck." He set the brush down and leaned back in the chair. He didn't know why this was such a big deal to him. Actually, that came out wrong. They were thinking about having a baby, making their family bigger. Of course it was a big deal, but what he didn't know was why the thought freaked him out so much.

Braden and Jessie were his world. He loved the girl with all his heart. She was a little piece of his sister that he would always have. Braden was his future, his soul mate. Nothing would ever change that.

He should be ecstatic over the idea of having a baby with him, and part of him was. Jesus, could he imagine a little kid out there running around with Braden's DNA? Wes smiled at the thought.

Would the baby look like Braden's family? Have the blond curls Jessie got from her mom?

More smiling.

But then he thought about Jessie. She was used to being an only child. She'd had all her mother's attention before she passed and now she was the center of Wes and Braden's world. They showered her with affection, probably spoiled her rotten, and all of that would change with another child in the house.

She'd lived through so much in her short life, losing both her parents so young, and Wes's main goal in life was to make Jessie's world as easy on her as he could. Would this make it harder on her or easier?

Before he realized it, hours had passed. He wasn't sure how he sat in front of a blank canvas thinking that long, but somehow he had.

Honestly, Wes never saw himself with kids. Ever. He'd been scared to death of screwing up Jessie's life when Chelle left her to him. All those same fears weighed him down again now.

What if he screwed up?

What if he made the wrong decision?

What if he didn't have what it took?

He wasn't any clearer on what he should do, but what he did know was that he needed his husband. Wes didn't want to do this alone.

He stood, his socked feet padding across the floor as he made his way to the door and opened it. The hallway was short. The TV played softly in the background. A fire crackled and popped in the fireplace...Braden was curled up on the couch asleep. He lay on his side, his back to the back of the couch. Wes walked over, his heart beating harder and faster with each step.

He studied the softness of Braden's expression while he slept. Traced the laugh lines on his face with his eyes. Wanted to run his fingers through Braden's soft hair because everything was easier when he had Braden in his arms. He made life seem simple, yet so much *more* at the same time.

They could do this. Together they could do anything, couldn't they?

Wes climbed onto the couch beside him. Braden's arms immediately wrapped around him. It was a tight fit, but they made it work, tangling their legs together, molding as close to each other's bodies as they could. "Mmm…Missed you," Braden mumbled softly without opening his eyes.

"I missed you, too."

"Take a nap with me, Wesley," his words were sleep-slurred and somehow sexy on top of it. "Rest that brain and heart of yours. We'll figure it out."

Wes relaxed, closed his eyes, and did exactly what Braden said.

WHEN WES WOKE up, the room was completely dark except for the dim fire hardly burning and the muted TV. He pulled far enough away from Braden to look at his face, only to see the man staring back at him.

"There's a wrinkle in your forehead that wasn't there when you were sleeping. Stop being so serious." Braden brushed his thumb over Wes's skin as though he could straighten out the wrinkle.

"I didn't know I was thinking too much."

"You always are."

Wes leaned up on his elbow and looked down at Braden who smiled. "If we have a baby, you won't be the biggest kid in the house anymore."

Braden barked out a laugh at that, making Wes smile. He loved it when he made Braden laugh. The guy had the best sense of humor of anyone he knew and it felt good to be the one to put a smile on his face.

"I didn't think about that. We all know Jess is the oldest one of us all. I changed my mind. No baby Jensen-Roth for us." But then the smile in his green eyes turned serious, heartfelt. Maybe a little sad. It made Wes's breath catch because he realized the bone-deep want inside Braden for this.

"I think we'd be good daddies to a little baby. You'd be there to make sure I didn't fuck up. I'd let them stay up too late and drink too much milk and teach them fart jokes when they were too young. Then Jessie would show us how it should be done."

Wes had to admit, when Braden spoke like that, it sounded nice. He couldn't help but smile. "Jesus, we'd be in so much trouble with a little baby with your DNA. I've heard your parents' stories about you. I'd have gray hair in no time."

"Oooh." Braden leaned forward and kissed him. "Silver foxes are hot."

"Shut the fuck up." Wes playfully shoved Braden and then sat up. His husband did the same, their legs touching. Wes couldn't stop his mind from running away from him, from focusing on all the shit that could make this difficult for them. What if it upset Jessie? What if Lizzy had a problem carrying the baby? What if he was a shitty father to a second child? Sometimes he felt like he was just getting a handle on things with Jessie. He still worried about screwing up every fucking day and with another kid that would be doubled.

"Don't close me out. Let me in. Tell me what's going on in that head of yours." Braden reached out and rubbed his thumb over Wes's temple…and it helped. Braden always helped.

"I won't close you out. Never again. You know that. I just…I'm scared, Braden. I'm scared to death of screwing up two kids' lives. I'm scared we'll have a baby, because Christ, I think I want to have one with you, and it's the wrong thing to do. That we end up hurting Jessie or the baby, or, fuck, I don't know."

"You think I'm not scared? Hell, I have a jar full of money at home that I keep filling up because I curse too much, and I let Jess eat her snack too late when you're not home, and we watch too much Tom and Jerry. I don't do anything by the book, not like I'm supposed to but...I love her. I love her so much it fucking hurts. I'd do anything for her just like you would. We have so much love between us, Wesley. That's all that matters. We love our kids and everything else will turn out just fine."

When Braden said something, it was virtually impossible for Wes not to believe him.

-7-

AND THAT WAS enough seriousness for a little while. Regardless of what they decided or if they even made a decision this weekend, Braden wanted their time together to be about them as well.

"Sugar and coffee for old time's sake?" he asked and then Wes cocked a brow at him, a half grin on his face.

"The first time it was sex, then sugar and coffee."

"I'm willing to have sex with you any time, any place, so that's your call. I just have a sweet tooth and you know it. I think we should stay up all night. We slept half the day anyway. We can pretend we're not old and we don't have to drink a shit-ton of caffeine to stay awake until the sun rises." Another memory. They'd sat up all night on the porch and watched the sunrise when they were first getting to know each other. They had so many good memories together.

Wes nudged him. "I don't know who you're calling old, but it better not be me."

"Weren't we just talking about you being my silver fox?"

"I'm in my early thirties you asshole! You keep talking like that and I'm going to feel like I have to hit my midlife crisis and trade you in for a newer model."

Braden crawled over him, straddling Wes's lap as Wes leaned back to give Braden space. "You keep talking like that and I'm going to lock you away to make sure no one can have their way with you except me."

"Promise?" Wes winked at him.

"Abso-fucking-lutely. Now get the fire going while I get us

something sweet to eat." Braden leapt off his lap, fighting Wes's hold when he tried to pull Braden back down again.

"I don't want to move," Wes said.

"Get your ass up, Wesley. Coffee, sugar, and then sex. The longer you take the more time passes until we can get to the fucking."

Wes shoved to his feet. "Well, when you put it like that..."

"That's what I want to hear. Get it warm in here so we can get naked, too," Braden told him and then made his way into the kitchen. He heard Wes grumbling to himself, while he got the fire going again, mock-complaining about Braden being a slave driver.

Braden pulled out the tray of cinnamon rolls he'd special-requested, and then put them in the oven. Next came the coffee.

The whole time his mind was in the next room with his husband. Wes was scared. He'd known he would be. He didn't deal well with change. He'd always worry in some ways that he wasn't enough, or about outside factors they couldn't control, and Braden wondered if part of that had to do with his dad leaving. Wes had always felt like he would lose people he loved—first his dad, then his mom, then Chelle.

Jessie had owned his heart from the start. Then Braden barreled his way into Wes's life and made Wes risk his heart with Braden as well. Now, he was asking Wes to risk it a third time on a new baby.

He'd never known when to leave well enough alone and Braden sure as shit didn't plan to start now. This would make their life complete.

When the oven dinged he pulled the tray out, transferred the rolls to a plate and then filled two cups of coffee, making it how they liked it. He grabbed the cups first and made his way back into the living room to see the fire roaring and a pallet of blankets on the floor in front of it. "Check you out. If this isn't the sweetest fucking thing in the world, I don't know what is. You didn't have to go to all this trouble. I already told you I'd put out."

Wes mock-rolled his eyes at him. "Like I'd doubt that, you little slut."

"I'm a slut for you." Braden nodded toward the kitchen. "Want to grab the food?"

"Sure thing." He and Wes passed each other on their way. Braden set the cups on the floor and then pulled the coffee table close to them, before putting them on the table.

"Cinnamon rolls?" Wes's voice held a soft, nostalgic tone to it that matched the way Braden felt. "That was the night we went out. I got too drunk and passed out on you, so you left." Wes walked over, set the food on the table and then joined Braden on the pallet. "You set up the coffee pot for me so I just had to push start. I think that's when it really hit me how special you are."

Braden reached over and grabbed one of the sticky cinnamon rolls. "Well I am incredibly sweet. Hot as fuck, too."

"Who could doubt that?" Wes winked at him. "You're also not holding back on being sentimental."

No, he wasn't, and Braden wasn't going to apologize for that. "We've had some good years, Wesley. Now we can make completely new memories."

Wes's brows pulled together, that wrinkle making an appearance on his forehead again. "You're still happy though, right? I know you're used to adventure, packing up and leaving when you want or finding trouble to get into. I need to know that's not what this is… That you want to move forward and grow our family because it's something you want for us and not because you need something new and exciting."

Braden flinched at Wes's words. A pain shot through his chest and his first response was to be hurt…and then pissed. But as he looked into Wes's thoughtful hazel eyes, saw the concern there, the love, he couldn't be angry. Not really. Wes was being responsible. He wasn't just jumping without thinking everything through like Braden had been known to do. This wasn't a spontaneous idea—he'd had months to think it through.

"I don't want to make it sound like I doubt you. Jesus, I hope that didn't come out wrong. I know you love us. I just…"

"It's a valid question, but I think you already know the answer to it. I hope you do, at least. You know me, Wesley. You know if I'm happy or not." To distract himself, Braden pinched a bite off of the cinnamon roll and ate it.

"You're right. I take it back. I know who you are and how you feel."

That was the exact answer Braden needed to hear.

-8-

WES LAY ON the pallet watching the fire. Braden had gone to take a shower, or to give Wes some time on his own—probably a mixture of both.

It was close to dawn now. They'd eaten cinnamon rolls, drank coffee and talked for hours. It wasn't often they spent time like that, or at least not hours of it. They laughed daily. That was a given when you lived with Braden, but this? Tonight? It was as though they had all the time in the world just to be with each other. There was no rushing to work, or getting Jess to school or making sure they were around for piano lessons. Sure, they'd spent most of their time chatting about Jessie—her last piano recital, Braden's visit to her school for parent's career day (having a fireman for a parent made her a hit), and when she talked to her class on Father's Day about how cool it was to have two dads.

They talked about everything, even the more difficult times.

Jessie still had times where she cried because she missed her mom. Wes would miss his sister every day of his life. There were arguments and worries and wondering if they were raising Jessie the way Chelle would want them to…but he knew they were. In his heart he knew that.

His heart also knew that Chelle had always wished for a big family for her girl. That couldn't be his reasoning for having a baby, though. As much as he loved his sister, they had to do this because it was what was right for their family now. Right for Jessie, Braden and Wes as a whole.

Between Braden's family and Wes's, she had a big family in so many ways. Plus, Noah and Coop and Gavin and Mason who all treated her like the princess she wanted to be. She was probably the luckiest girl in the world with how many people she had loving her.

But there could never be enough love, could there?

What they were doing, reminiscing about the good times and talking about the struggles, they were reminding Wes that that was what life was all about: Living it. Not that he didn't know that. How could he not with Braden in his world? But sometimes you just had to stop and take the time to evaluate things. To look at the big picture—not the beginning of a painting. Not the sketch or the background, but the finished product as a whole, and see how fucking beautiful it was. But there's always room for more beauty. And even though things felt perfect, when it came to life and the people you loved, there were ways to add to the beauty of the life you already lived.

He heard a noise behind him and Wes rolled onto his back to see Braden walking toward him.

His dark hair was wet. Little droplets of water ran down the side of his face. He wasn't wearing a shirt, showing more pearls of leftover water on his skin. Wes wanted to lick every one of them. Wanted to taste every inch of Braden's body as though he'd never had the privilege. He wanted to devour him, and savor him at the same time.

His sweatpants rode low on his hips. He had that sexy, fucking "V" that Wes had traced with his tongue over and over and over. He would do it a million more times and never tire of it.

And then Braden smiled. His lips rose, showing a dimple, making his eyes wrinkle slightly around the edges. Wes's heart damn near stopped beating. This man, *his* man, was the most beautiful person in the world. Wes loved him so much, he ached with it.

"Take your sweats off."

Braden didn't hesitate to do exactly as Wes said. He pulled them off, his rigid, thick cock springing free. Wes wanted his face there, nestled in Braden's dark pubic hair. Wanted to inhale his scent. Wanted to taste his skin. Wanted to fuck him until he couldn't walk anymore. "Come here. Lay on me."

Braden smiled again, walked over and straddled Wes's hips. He smelled like their soap. Wes touched his sides, ran his hands up Braden's warm skin. "I want your mouth."

That was all it took for Braden to lean forward, to lie on top of him and give Wes what he asked for.

Wes was running the show. He devoured Braden's mouth, pushed his tongue in deep, sucked and nipped at Braden's lip. His hands found a home on Braden's tight ass, squeezed his muscular globes as Braden thrust their cocks together.

He really fucking wished he was naked right now, too.

They lay there making out for what felt like hours. Braden's hand was in his hair. Wes still held his ass as they rubbed off on one another, savoring, touching and kissing each other.

He wanted to experience everything with this man. He already thought he was so fucking lucky and that they had everything. And in some ways they did. They could be happy, they could thrive in their current family...but what was holding them back from having more?

Wes rolled, flipped them so that Braden lay on his back on their pallet.

"Mmm, you're a sexy motherfucker when you manhandle me like that. What do you want, Wesley? Take it from me. You can have anything. I'm all yours."

"I want everything," Wes said and then he devoured Braden's mouth again. They swallowed each other's moans. Braden shoved his hands down Wes's sweats, cupping his ass the same way Wes had done to him.

"What are you going to do to me?" Braden asked when Wes began kissing his neck. "Tell me how you're going to drive me wild. Drive me crazy with anticipation, until I can't fucking take it anymore."

Wes's cock twitched. His balls ached. He wanted to fucking come just from Braden's words. "First I'm going to blow you."

He kissed one of Braden's nipples. "Then I'm going to eat your hole." He made eye contact with Braden who gave him a simple nod, confirming that yes, he was ready for Wes. He kissed the other nipple. "Then I'm going to fuck you, gonna love you so good."

There was a swat on his ass and Braden said, "Get going then."

"Eenie." Wes began kissing his way down Braden's body. "Meenie." More kissing. "Miney." He stopped when he got to Braden's cock. It was nearly purple he was so hard, the veins pulsing in his thick shaft. "Moe."

"Copycat," Braden teased him. Braden had said the same thing to Wes when they were first fucking around.

"Do you have a problem with it?" Wes settled himself between Braden's legs, looking up at him, his mouth so fucking close to Braden's dick.

"No. You can say whatever you want. Just blow me."

Wes started at the root of Braden's erection, then ran his tongue up to the head. Braden hissed. Wes smiled. "My. Fucking. Pleasure." And then he took Braden's cock all the way to the back of his throat.

-9-

BRADEN CURSED, INTENSE pleasure burning through him as he sank his dick deep into Wes's hot, wet mouth. Each time Wes swallowed him down, his satisfaction coaxed another moan out of him. "So good. Fuck, you feel so good, Wesley."

Braden's eyes rolled back in his head. He saw fucking stars. He tightened his grip in Wes's hair as his husband relentlessly sucked him, greedy pull after greedy pull with his talented mouth.

Wes palmed his balls, played with his tight sac before his mouth left Braden's cock and went to his nuts to lick and suck at those as well.

Braden was delirious with pleasure.

His balls got tighter, filled to the point where he wasn't sure he could hold himself back from emptying them. "I'm gonna come. Fuck, Wesley I'm gonna come if you don't stop."

And he wasn't ready to shoot his load yet. He wanted this to last.

Wes's mouth pulled off of him with a pop. He shoved up, kicked out of his sweats and pulled his shirt over his head. "You can't come yet. It's too early."

Braden saw a pearl of pre-come at the tip of Wes's dick. He wanted it on his tongue. Braden sat up, grabbed Wes and leaned forward so he could suck him. He licked at the slit and was rewarded with more pre-come.

"Oh, fuck," Wes gritted out just as Braden pulled off of him.

"Sorry, just wanted to taste you. Carry on. Should I roll over so you can eat my ass now?"

Wes laughed, which made Braden smile.

"You're such a crazy sonofabitch. But yeah, roll over, I'm not done with you yet."

Braden rolled to his stomach, shoved a pillow from their pallet under himself, so his ass was higher and then spread his legs. "I'm waiting."

If he wasn't already lying down, Wes's grin would have knocked him on his ass.

"Goddamn, I love you."

"I love you too."

And then Wes was between his legs again. He spread Braden's cheeks wide, licked a path down his crack, and then blew on him. A tremor of pleasure rode down Braden's spine.

He thrust backward when suddenly Wes's face was there, right between his cheeks, his tongue running back and forth over Braden's tender hole.

"Yes…yes…" Braden's brain turned to mush. It was like the only word he knew was *yes*. Every once in a while he threw a *more* in there and when he did, Wes gave him exactly what he asked for.

He managed a, "What the fuck? Come back," when Wes pulled away, but his husband only pulled at Braden's body, getting him up on his hands and knees.

As soon as he was in position, Wes went at him again, the sweet burn of his facial hair, rubbing against his skin and adding to the delicious friction each time he moved.

His body ached. His hole clenched. He wanted more. "Get something inside me, Wesley, before I lose my fucking mind."

Braden thrust back, trying to get as close to Wes as he could. When Wes's hand was at his mouth, he knew exactly what the other man wanted. He sucked Wes's finger into his mouth, wetting it as Wes continued eating at his hole.

Seconds after his hand was gone, Braden felt pressure at his ring and then Wes's wet finger pushed inside him. There were a couple of quick thrusts, and a mumbled, "Fuck yes," from Braden before he added another finger—twisting and turning them, fucking Braden to stretch him.

When Wes curled his finger and rubbed his prostate, his arms almost gave out.

"You're so hot inside. I love feeling your tight hole around me," Wes said as he thrust his fingers in deep, pulled them almost out again before sliding them home.

Braden rode his hand, shoving himself back on Wes needing more. Wanting everything. And then his mouth was there again too, Wes's tongue lashing at his hole while his fingers fucked him.

He wanted to live in this moment…but he wanted more, too. "Gimme your cock. Want your dick inside of me. Make love to me, Wesley."

Wes moaned against his pucker. "Want inside you so fucking much. I didn't think this through very well." He kissed the cheek of Braden's ass, his fingers still buried deep. "I need to go get the lube."

"I thought it through for you. Pocket of my sweats," Braden said.

"We make a good team," Wes smiled.

"The best."

When Wes pulled his fingers free, he reached over for the sweats and Braden lay down. He knew he couldn't hold himself up anymore, not with Wes fucking him.

"On your back, Braden. I want to look at you."

Braden rolled over, spread his legs wide and pulled them close to his chest, giving himself to Wes.

"You are so beautiful." Wes wrapped his hand around Braden's cock and pumped once. "You are so mine."

And then Wes was there, between Braden's legs. He leaned in, his dick at Braden's aching hole. Wes lowered himself, lying on top of him and then he felt the sweet burn as Wes's crown breached his asshole. "Ohhh, fuck yessss."

Once he had the head inside, Wes thrust, filling him completely. A strangled shout came from Braden's lips, and at the same time a satisfied groan from Wes's throat as he buried himself inside.

When he looked down at Braden, Wes's eyes were filled with so much emotion, so much love. It was like a switch had been flipped. The fast went to slow, as he pulled out, and then eased his way deep again.

"Kiss me," Braden told him and Wes did. His tongue swept Braden's mouth in unison with each thrust. Braden held onto Wes, wrapped his arms around him tightly, touching and rubbing and holding him as they moved together.

"Such a tight, hot cave. I love being inside of you."

"Love having you inside of me," Braden answered, and he did. He let his hands roam downward. He clutched Wes's ass, urging him on. Each time Wes thrust he tried to get him closer, as close as they could get. Braden sucked Wes's tongue into his mouth, and Wes's hand knotted in Braden's hair. They were sweating, their bodies slapping together as they made love.

Each time they rocked together, his dick rubbed against Wes's hard abs, the hair of his trail adding to the friction.

The tingle at the base of his spine got stronger. As if he knew, Wes thrust harder, deeper, maybe deeper than he'd ever gone. Braden's balls were heavy, aching for release.

"Love me hard. Make me come," Braden whispered between kisses.

Wes leaned back slightly, holding himself over Braden and began thrusting in earnest, each one more powerful and intense than the last. Their eyes never left each other's.

"Fuck...I'm gonna come, Braden. I'm ready to explode over here."

His body smacked hard against Braden's as Braden gave into his orgasm, his whole body going up in flames. He came in spurt after spurt, come roping up his body to his neck. His hole clenched, Wes tensed, and then he felt Wes's hot come shoot deep inside him, *once, twice.* When Wes thrust a third time, he held still, buried all the way to the hilt and finished emptying himself inside of Braden.

"So fucking good," he said and then leaned forward, licking away the evidence of Braden's orgasm from his body. It was the hottest fucking thing he'd ever experienced.

When Wes lowered himself on top of him, his deflating cock still inside of Braden, slowly easing its way out, Braden knew that whatever happened, he would still be the happiest fucking man in the world.

-10-

BRADEN'S HAND MOVED up and down Wes's back. He closed his eyes, concentrating on Braden's touch. Their breathing matched; he felt Braden's inhale and exhale against his own chest. It was the perfect moment.

"I wore ya out, huh? I think my ass has magical powers. It can bring down the toughest of men."

And now the moment was even more perfect because Braden lay beneath him, being one hundred percent himself, despite the fact that he didn't know what Wes would want to do.

Wes chuckled. "Are you sure it's just your ass? I mean, what about your mouth when you suck me off? Your dick when you fuck me? Or is it just you?"

Braden nodded. "You're right. I don't know what I was thinking. I'm just fucking magical all the way around." His hand still moved up and down Wes's back. They were both sticky, sweaty, with come between them, just the way they liked it.

And then he cupped Wes's face, one of his fingers rubbing the side of Wes's head, close to his eye. "You look tired. Your eyes are bloodshot; your eyebrows are furrowed. Turn your brain off, Wesley."

But he couldn't. Not that easily. He might never be able to completely. And he was tired, exhausted. Braden had to be too, but...

"You want to go home early?"

Jesus this man knew him so well. Inside and out. "I think so." He wanted to see Jess. Talk to her. He missed their girl.

"Yeah...yeah, me too. How about we take an hour nap to

take the edge off. That way she can sleep in a little, and then we'll head back. I suddenly feel like being home, too."

So that's what they did. Braden set the alarm on his phone and then they slept, wrapped all around each other right there on their pallet on the floor. When the alarm went off, they cleaned their mess in the cabin, made coffee, showered and got ready to leave, even though they were supposed to be there an extra day.

Neither of them spoke much. No doubt they were both deep in thought. It wasn't long before they were climbing back into the truck and heading back to Blackcreek, Wes driving this time.

Braden called Lydia from the road so she knew they were coming. A couple of hours later when they opened her front door, Wes stumbled backward a few feet as a little body crashed into him. He swept Jessie into his arms just as she said, "You're hooooome!" as though they'd been gone for weeks. "Did you have fun? I knew you were going but Braden said it was a secret! I did well and didn't tell you." She slipped sometimes, going back and forth between just calling Braden by his name, and putting the "Daddy" in front of it. They both were of the mind that she could call them whatever she wanted—dad, uncle, or by their names and they would respect it.

"You did real well, kiddo. I had no idea." Wes kissed her cheek and held her as her little arms wrapped around him. When Chelle had died and left Jessie to him, he was so damn scared of screwing up. He still was, but now he focused more on just how lucky he was to be loved by such a special kid. How lucky he was to have her depend on him and make him laugh and hug him. How lucky he was to share all of that with the man beside him.

"Why'd you come home early?" she asked.

"Because we missed you."

"Yeah, Squirt. It's not the same without you." Braden ruffled her curls and she giggled.

"That's cuz I'm awesome!"

Both Wes and Braden let out a loud laugh at that. Wes knew exactly whose influence made things like that come out of her mouth.

"You are," Wes told her and then looked over her shoulder at Braden who sheepishly shrugged. It was amazing how much like Braden she was.

They had a quick conversation with Lydia and the rest of the family before the three of them were climbing into the truck to head home.

"Are we going to Cooper and Noah's to get the dogs?" Jessie asked from the cab.

Wes opened his mouth to say yes, but Braden cut him off. "Nope. I'm going to drop you and your dad off at home. I have some things I need to take care of and then afterward, I'll get the monsters and bring them home to you."

"Okay," Jessie replied as Wes looked at Braden. His husband winked at him, before returning his eyes to the road, having gotten into the driver's seat after their stop at Lydia's. Wes reached over and squeezed his leg, a quiet thank you for knowing Wes wanted some time with Jessie.

Braden kept the truck idling as they pulled up at their house, the house Jess used to share with her mom. Would they need to get another room if they had a baby? It wasn't fair to ask Jessie to share. Maybe Wes could move his painting studio from the third room into his and Braden's. He was sure they could find space there.

He would do it, he realized. He would do whatever he needed to if this happened... If they had a baby. Because he was pretty sure he wanted that. But only if the little girl in the backseat was okay with it, too.

"Don't get into too much trouble without me." Braden's words pulled Wes from his thoughts.

"Somehow I don't think we're the ones you should worry about." And then Wes leaned in and pressed a quick kiss to Braden's mouth. "Thank you."

"Anything. Always." Braden winked at him before turning toward the cab. "I'll see you soon, Squirt. Make sure your dad records Tom and Jerry so we can watch it when I get back."

Wes couldn't help but smile. Braden made even the mundane seem fresh and exciting. Their lives were so much better for having him in it.

"Bye, Daddy Braden. Love you!" Jessie said and Wes's heart squeezed. He would never tire of hearing that.

"Love you, too. Have some hot chocolate for me!"

Wes helped Jessie out of the truck. The two of them made their way through the snow and to the house before Braden drove away.

He did exactly as Braden said and made them two mugs of hot chocolate with lots of marshmallows, which were Jessie's favorite. After he set the DVR to record their show, he called Jessie from her room. "Do you want to hang out for a little while?" he asked her.

"No." She shook her head and Wes felt his eyes bulge. Jessie started laughing. "I'm teasing, silly!"

He dropped his head back not sure whether to laugh or cry. "You are exactly like Braden, do you know that?"

"Thank you!" Jessie grinned at him and then the two of them sat on the floor around the coffee table with their mugs. "Where'd you guys go?" she asked.

"To a cabin to hang out. It's Mason's. He let us borrow it. Did you have fun with Aunt Lydia and your cousins?"

Jessie nodded, melted marshmallow on her upper lip. "Yep. How come you guys left? Was it a date?"

Oh, this girl. He didn't know what they were going to do with her. "Kind of. Braden just wanted to do something nice for me as a surprise. How are you doing? Everything's okay with you?" Both he and Braden checked in with her often to make sure things were going well. They were big with communication, asking questions and talking about her mom. They also wanted to make sure she had no problems at school and luckily, she hadn't.

"Uh huh. I started my list for Santa. Aunt Lydia said twenty-two more days until Christmas. Are we going to Grandma and

Grandpa's?" She meant Braden's parents. They'd been swapping back and forth each year between spending Christmas day with Lydia or with the Roth clan.

"I think we're going to head that way late Christmas Eve. Noah and Cooper are having a Christmas Eve party that we're going to." Cooper insisted on it, though that was like Coop. When he got something in his head, he intended to get it, and Noah usually made damn sure he did. "It works out well for everyone this year so we're going to celebrate a big Christmas with your Grandma and Grandpa but we won't get to their house until very late. We made sure Santa knows to come late." He was so thankful for Braden's family. They took Jessie in like their own. His parents were the only grandparents she had.

"Okay!" Jessie shrugged and then took another sip of her cocoa.

Wes's stomach twisted. His heart thudded and he suddenly felt hot. "I have a question for you. I want you to tell me how you really feel, no matter what, okay? You don't have to worry about saying the wrong thing or anything like that."

Jessie nodded, more interested in her drink and the marshmallows.

"This is just a question for now, okay? I know it's confusing but there's no guarantee this will happen. I just want to see how you feel about it."

She looked up at him then, her eyes sweet and confused.

"Come here," Wes told her. When she stood up, he pulled her to his lap, encircling his arms around her. "How would you feel about being a big sister?"

She turned to look at him, her brows furrowed the way Wes knew his own often did. "I thought two boys couldn't have babies?"

Wes's heart sank to his stomach. He wasn't excited about having these talks. "Wait. What do you know about that?"

The confusion on her face grew. "Nothin'. Just that girls have babies in their bellies."

He let out a deep breath, embarrassed he'd almost lost his mind over something so innocent. "They do, but there are also ways two men can have a baby. They can adopt a baby or another woman can carry it in her belly for them."

"How?"

Um...this wasn't something he really wanted to explain, nor did he really know how. He hadn't anticipated these kinds of questions, though he should have. "It's just something doctors can do. I promise I'll explain it someday. What's important right now is how you would feel if there was a baby in the house. That means things would change. Braden and I would still love you with all our hearts, but we'd have another child to love, too."

"Could I help take care of the baby?"

"Yes."

"Would the baby sleep in my room? I don't want it to mess up my stuff."

Wes held in a laugh. "No, the baby wouldn't sleep in your room."

"Would we still get to do fun stuff together, and Braden would still take me bowling and we'd watch Tom and Jerry and play outside and you and Daddy Braden would still paint my nails?"

Wes smiled at her. "Yes, all of that would still happen. We'll always love you just as much as we do now. And we'll always want to spend time with you. You'll always be our girl, just the way you'll always be your mama's girl."

She looked down at that and Wes wondered if he said the wrong thing. If maybe he shouldn't have brought Chelle into it, but then, he wanted his sister to play a big role in Jessie's life even though she wasn't here. He wanted Jessie to always know how much her mom loved her.

"Mommy liked babies."

"She did. She was so happy when she found out she was having you. She loved you more than anyone else in the world."

"I like playing with Quinn. He's fun." Quinn was the youngest of one of Braden's sisters. He hadn't thought of that, how much Jessie loved to play with Quinn. How excited she was to see the baby each time they went.

"He is fun. Babies are a lot of work, too. It won't always be perfect, but it could be special." His baby with Braden. Jessie's sibling. Their family of three (or five if you counted the dogs) growing. He liked the sound of that more and more.

"I could tell the baby what to do!" Jessie said and Wes bit back a laugh.

"Well, the baby wouldn't do much of anything at first. And you'd have to be fair but yes, you'll be older and that comes with certain perks."

Jessie curled her little fingers in his shirt. "I would be a good sister."

"The best."

"Just like you and Braden are the best dads!"

Wes squeezed her tight, held her, this girl that they loved so much. This girl who thought both he and Braden hung the moon. They held each other for a few minutes. Wes touched her curls and thought of his sister. He wasn't going to push this. Jessie could answer him whenever she wanted to—today, tomorrow, next week, next month. And he knew Braden would feel the same.

"Daddy?" she said a few minutes later.

"Yeah."

"Does that mean I can take a baby off my Christmas list for Santa and add something else since you and Braden are asking him for one?"

Wes's chest swelled. His smile stretched so big his cheeks hurt. It was the perfect fucking answer, and so incredibly Jessie he didn't know how he didn't see it coming. "Yeah, kiddo. Yeah, you can take a baby off your Christmas list. We have it under control."

-11-

BRADEN DIDN'T HAVE anything to do. He'd been full of shit when he said that to Jessie so he made his way to the firehouse, hung out there for a bit, and then was about to go see what Mason was up to at the bar when his phone beeped with a text.

Meet Jess and me at the bridge. We're going for a walk.

A walk in the snow sounded like an awesome time to him…kind of. The company sounded good, though, so Braden replied with an **Okay** and then turned his truck around and headed for a small park on the other side of town. A creek went through the middle of it, a small bridge crossing, with trees all around it. It wasn't a place they spent a great deal of time, but there was a large Christmas tree in the middle of the park that the town lit every year, starting on the first.

It was too early in the day for the lights, but he knew Jess liked looking at it anyway.

When he got there, Wes and Jessie were standing by the car. She was bundled up as though they were in the middle of an active blizzard, but that was Wes. Always cautious.

"You're slooooow. What took you so long?" Jessie asked hugging him.

"Slow? What are you talking about, Squirt? I hit the nitro in the truck so it would practically fly here."

Her blonde brows knitted together. "What's nitro?"

Braden shook his head. "Nothing. Come on, let's go play."

The three of them went to the open grassy area covered in a

layer of snow. They had snowball fights, looked at the Christmas tree, talked about Cooper's Christmas Eve party, and then spoke about going to Braden's family's house, too.

Braden didn't ask questions, waiting for Wes to approach him with whatever he had to say when he was ready. They weren't there for long when Jessie asked, "Can we walk to the bridge?"

"Yep. Sure thing, kid. Let's go," Braden told her.

She jogged ahead of them as they headed in that direction. Wes reached over and grabbed his hand. "Needed to touch me, huh? I'll keep you warm if you need it." Braden pulled him closer.

"I can keep myself warm, thank you very much," Wes replied with laughter in his voice.

Jessie was on the other side of the small bridge by the time they made it halfway over. Playground equipment was on the other side. They could see it through the snow-covered trees. "Can I go play?" she asked.

"Stay close," Wes called back to her.

Wes looked out over the side of the bridge and to the water beneath them. Braden's arm touched his as he stood next to him waiting. His gut was a knot of uncertainty. He wanted this, wanted it so fucking much.

"I wanna have a baby with you," Wes said after a few beats of silence. "Let's do it."

Just that quickly the tangle in Braden's stomach loosened. He could breathe when he didn't realize his chest had been tight before. They were going to do this. They were going to make Jessie a big sister. They were going to have a fucking kid. "Not sure we have the right equipment for that."

"Funny man." Wes turned to him and Braden did the same. "I'm scared out of my mind and this is a big step. Our whole lives are going to change, Braden. I didn't plan on having one kid and now we're going to try and have a second...but I want that. With you. I want a little kid with Roth DNA. I want to see how much like you they are, because you shine so bright, even Jess is exactly like you."

Jesus, he loved his man. "I hope the baby is like you. Strong and honorable. The type of person who would do anything for someone they love." That was his Wesley.

"Are we really going to do this? Are we really going to have your sister carry a baby for us?"

Braden nodded. "We are. Holy shit, we so fucking are, Wesley."

Despite having a loving family that he adored, Braden had never really felt roots, never really felt tied to something or someone until this man stepped into his life. They fell in love. They changed each other's worlds. They were a family. They raised an incredible little girl together…and now they were going to try and make that family bigger. "I love you, Wesley."

"I love you too."

Braden cupped Wes's face with his gloved hands, and leaned in to kiss him. This was the best gift anyone could ever give him.

He couldn't wait to see what the future held for them, for his family.

GAVIN
&
MASON

-1-

GAVIN DAVIS COULDN'T be happier about Christmas break. He loved his job. He was thankful for it every day. He got to share his love of music. He got to show children the beauty in it and hope they would love it the way he did…but yeah, thank God for having the holidays off. He and every other teacher he knew needed that break, just as he was sure most parents were at least a little bit thankful when the break was over. Kids were great, but he was ready for a vacation.

Or at least, ready to trade in teaching for bartending with his partner, Mason, if you called that a vacation.

Gavin did.

He loved working at Creekside with Mason. Maybe that was because it brought back memories of how they'd fallen in love…or it could just be the fact that his lover was a kinky bottom who wasn't averse to sneaking into the back office as much as possible…

As Gavin stood from his desk, his phone buzzed. He pulled it from his pocket and headed for the door. "Hey, Braden," he said to his oldest friend.

"Wes and I are going to try and have a baby."

A smile stretched across his face at the announcement. "I wasn't aware that you guys had the right parts for that," he teased as Braden's loud laughter sounded through the phone. It took his friend a minute to settle down. "I'm not that funny so I'm guessing there's a story I don't know to go along with that." Gavin made his way out of the building and to his car. He shivered as he hit the button to open the door. It was a cold winter, snow already covering the ground.

"Nothing. It's similar to what Wes said when I brought it up to him at the cabin. We decided to go for it right away, but we've been sitting on the news for a week or so."

Ah, so that's what their weekend at Mason's cabin had been about. He should have known it was something along those lines. Braden was thriving, having latched onto family life in a way that Gavin never would have seen coming when they were teenagers.

"Lizzy's going to carry the baby for us. We have our first appointment with the doctor next week!" Braden's excitement practically seeped through the line. Gavin's pulse sped up and a small grin stretched across his face. It felt good to see how happy his friend was. It felt good to be equally happy and in love himself.

"That's exciting, man. I'm happy for you guys." Gavin continued chatting with Braden while he waited for his car to warm up.

"What are you up to this weekend?" Braden asked, just as Gavin had been about to tell him he had to go.

"I'm heading home now. I'm going to clean up and change before I go to work with Mason tonight. Weekends are busy, and since I'm on break he eased up on his help so we can work together. I'm playing at the bar tomorrow night. If you and Wes can get a babysitter you guys should come down. I think Noah and Cooper are coming."

"We're planning on it. Your boyfriend already told us. Jess is having a sleepover with a friend."

Gavin smiled at that. He wasn't surprised Mason made sure everyone knew he'd be performing at Creekside. It wasn't something Gavin did very often because of work and being busy, but when he did, Mason always made a big deal out of it. You'd think Gavin was performing for a crowd of thousands at the Pepsi Center. "He's so damn crazy. He acts like it's a big deal, like I'm not just playing in his bar. I'm just some guy playing at his boyfriend's establishment. It's not like he could turn me away even if he wanted to."

"Nah, he loves you. He's proud of you. Plus, musicians are sexy."

They both laughed, the comment from his friend not surprising Gavin in the least...and actually making him miss Mason at the same time. Every day he considered himself so damn lucky that the man loved him. They were different in a lot of ways, but those differences connected them. "Okay, I'm going to run. I'll see you tomorrow night. Congrats again."

"Thanks, man. I'll see you later."

Gavin tossed his cell phone onto the seat beside him and drove toward the home he shared with Mason. A little over a year ago they'd moved out of the house he'd bought from Braden and purchased a new place of their own. It was somewhat bigger, making it easier to fit a piano in the living room, where he gave lessons. He also had a music room that was about double the size of the one in the old place and Gavin used that to his advantage. His piano from Mason wasn't for anyone to touch other than them, so he kept that one in his private space.

His trip home was quick. He ate, showered, and changed before heading to Creekside.

As soon as he opened the door, Mason looked up at him from behind the bar and grinned. The man's smile lit up the room, and he knew it.

"Hey, Gavin," a few of the regulars said as he made his way to the bar. Gavin returned their hellos but kept moving toward Mason.

He made his way around the bar and stopped right in front of Mason. "Hey, Music Man. It's good to see you," Mason said. He leaned forward and pressed a quick kiss to Gavin's lips, then bent close to his ear, whispering, "I haven't properly scandalized you in a while. Think anyone will notice if we disappear and you get on your knees for me?"

Gavin chuckled and playfully pushed at Mason's shoulder. "Always horny."

"And you're not? If that's the case, I'm doing something wrong."

Mason winked at him and Gavin suddenly needed to kiss him again. He put a hand on his waist and leaned forward once more, their lips pressing together. "You're not doing a damn thing wrong."

"That's what I like to hear," Mason replied just as someone from down the bar cut in, "That's enough you two. My beer's empty. If I don't have anyone to kiss, I should at least be able to get drunk."

A group of them laughed, Gavin and Mason included. He'd never envisioned this kind of life for himself before. He'd been a proper school teacher with religious parents, hiding who he was.

That wasn't the life he had to live anymore. The man in front of him taught him he could have it all, and Gavin savored every second of it.

"You're spacing off. Get the man a beer." Mason popped him with a towel and Gavin rolled his eyes.

Yeah, life was good. He couldn't imagine it getting much better than this.

-2-

JESUS, IT HAD been a long night. Mason had no idea if half the town was celebrating being on winter break or what, but Creekside hadn't been that busy in a while. He enjoyed it, though. Mason had always loved working hard and when he could experience that side-by-side with Gavin, it was even more enjoyable. He got to laugh and joke with the man he loved while spending time in the bar he loved, too. It was a win-win. Especially because Gavin could pretend Mason scandalized him when he teased him in public. They both loved every second of it.

After wiping down the tables, he finished cleaning up while Gavin was in his office going over paperwork. He liked to try and help, even though the business aspect wasn't really his thing. Mason thought it was cute so he'd let him and then go over it and clean up any mistakes if he made them. They made a great team.

When Mason finished, he turned to yell for Gavin to come out, but something made him head back to the office instead. Okay, so he knew what it was that made him go that way. They shared a lot of memories in that office. He liked seeing Gavin in the space.

Mason stepped into the room to see his partner sitting in the chair behind the desk. He held a piece of paper in his hands, studying it intensely. His eyes squinted which was something they always did when Gavin was deep in thought. His nose wrinkled and Mason had to fight to hold in a laugh. Jesus, the man was cute.

"Are you trying not to laugh at me?" Gavin asked as though

he could read Mason's mind.

"You look so studious. Like the good, proper man that I want to ravage and get very, very bad with." Which honestly was one of his favorite things in the world to do—properly scandalize his schoolteacher boyfriend.

Gavin peeked at him over the edge of the paper, cocking a brow. His dark blond hair still hung slightly off the side of his forehead, and Christ, that fucking jawline of his. It was like the man was etched from stone.

Any chance of not having at least one part of Gavin right then and there flew out the window when the man smiled at him. It was such a sexy, shy smile. "Unbutton and unzip your pants," Mason told him, taking long strides into the office. He didn't bother closing the door. They were alone, everything was all locked up, and you couldn't see the office from the front windows.

Gavin dropped the paper. It fluttered to the floor before he quickly did as he was told. He was good at that when it came to sex—listening. And yeah, Mason loved that about him. Mason was a bottom all the way. He wanted to be fucked, not do the fucking, but that didn't mean he didn't want to be in charge. He always loved topping from the bottom and it worked for what Gavin needed, too.

"Where do you want me?" Gavin asked as he finished opening the fly on his jeans.

"Right where you are will do. Just pull your pants down a little bit so I can get to your cock and balls. That's all I need right now."

Gavin leaned back in the chair, raising his hips so he could pull his jeans partway down. His dick stood high, proud, that same color hair from his head a trimmed patch around the root. Mason wanted his lips stretched around his partner's thick erection so bad he could taste it—taste the salt on his body. He could feel the soft skin covering steel against his tongue before he even dropped to his knees between Gavin's legs.

Gavin looked down at him, lust brewing in his hooded eyes. It was hard not to return the smile when their eyes met. He loved seeing this man and knowing he was his. "Feed it to me."

He saw Gavin shudder, wondered if his balls drew up tighter. If they ached with the same need that filled Mason's. If he had the same throb in his crotch that Mason did.

"My pleasure." Gavin grabbed the root of his dick, angling it toward Mason's mouth. Mason opened wide for him, eased closer as Gavin pushed his crown past Mason's lips. He swirled his tongue around him, tasted the pre-come there, and then lowered his head to swallow his guy down.

"Ahhh...fuck yessss. I needed this," Gavin hissed out, his voice lustful and husky.

He threaded his fingers through Mason's hair, pulling slightly as Mason worked his cock with his mouth. He took him as deep as he could before pulling off and running his tongue from the tip to the base. "Mmm, I love the way you taste."

Gavin looked down at him, his eyes dark and stormy with need, and Mason said, "I love the feel of you in my mouth. Been wanting to drink your come all day. Now I want to make it last."

"Oh, fuck." Gavin's body visibly tensed. "You say stuff like that to me and it definitely won't last. Put me back in your mouth, Mase. Please."

"Since you asked so nicely." Mason bobbed his head over Gavin's lap again, sucking and licking at his thick, hard rod. Every so often he'd ease off, tracing the veins on Gavin's cock with his tongue, as he palmed his guy's heavy balls.

Gavin's hips started to move, thrusting forward and fucking Mason's mouth. His own dick seeped in his jeans, fucking ached, he needed to let loose so badly. He didn't stop sucking, didn't even screw up the rhythm as he unbuttoned and unzipped his pants. He pulled his dick out, wrapped a hand around it and started to jerk off.

Mason closed his lips tighter around Gavin's shaft. Sucked harder, faster, took him deeper. He felt the muscles in Gavin's legs tense. Heard his breathing quicken. There was an increase in the "Oh yeahs" and moaning above him and he knew Gavin would fill his mouth at any second.

Mason tugged harder on his own erection. Took Gavin to the back of his throat and swallowed around the head of his dick.

"Yes. Fuck yeah," Gavin groaned just as thick come shot from him, sliding down the back of Mason's throat. He spurted again and again, Mason still jerking his own cock, still sucking Gavin. The burn in his balls ignited. His sac tightened and then he shot all over his own hand in three long jets.

He hardly had a chance to take a breath when Gavin asked. "Can I have it?"

Oh yeah, Gavin had definitely grown since they'd been together and Mason loved every second of experiencing it with him. He put his fingers up to Gavin's mouth, letting him suck Mason's semen from his hand. When his fingers were clean, he wrapped his arms around Gavin's waist, resting his head in his lover's lap, Gavin's flaccid cock just inches away.

He loved everything about this man—making love with him, sucking him, holding him, working with him, talking to him. He loved listening to him play music, seeing the passion for his craft in Gavin's eyes.

"That felt good," Gavin said, running a hand through Mason's hair. "See? I told you, you're so damn horny all the time."

"Are you complaining?"

"Not a chance."

Mason had experienced a lot of sex in his life, but none of it held a candle to what it was like being with Gavin. He guessed that's what happened when you loved someone. They made everything better just by being there.

Again, seeming to read Mason's mind, Gavin said, "I love you," still playing with Mason's hair.

"I love you, too." There was nothing he wanted more than to spend the rest of his life showing Gavin just how much he loved him.

-3-

MASON WAS STILL passed out when Gavin woke up. He had a hard time sleeping in even though he'd been at Creekside late last night. Even though he wasn't much of a morning person, his internal clock was used to getting up early for school. That's just the way it was for him now. He couldn't deny that it was probably also the fact that he was performing tonight.

He loved being on stage. Loved playing his guitar or piano. The singing stressed him out, though he enjoyed that from time to time too, but no matter how much he enjoyed it all, the nerves were always there.

Really, he was happy about that. Nerves meant he cared and he never wanted to get over feeling that way about music.

Realizing there was no way he could go back to sleep, he kissed Mason's cheek. The man didn't move a muscle, not even when Gavin ran a hand over his bare ass before covering him up.

He pulled on a pair of sweats and a T-shirt before leaving the room. He made some coffee, waited for it to finish brewing and then took a mug of it into his music room. His stomach twisted and turned more than it usually did before taking the stage. Gavin chalked it up to having not performed in a while.

He needed to call and check in on his mom, but it was still a little too early for that. About six months before, his father had passed away. It was hard on them both, but at least they knew he wasn't suffering anymore. Dementia had eaten at his mind to the point that the last few months of his life had been extremely emotional and painful for all of them. They knew his father wouldn't have wanted to live that way – he was at peace now.

Even though his dad had been in a home for quite a while, losing him had changed his relationship with his mom. Gavin checked on her a lot more often now, even if it was only a phone call every other day.

Despite how long he and Mason had been together, she still struggled with their relationship because of her faith. She wanted to support them, and ever since a conversation between Gavin and his dad in one of his lucid moments, she tried, but it was an internal battle for her.

Still, the three of them had dinner together once in a while and she made it a habit to ask about Mason from time to time. Most of the time when he went to see her he went alone, and she had yet to make the visit to Blackcreek to see them or their home, and she definitely didn't approve of Mason's bar.

He figured that might be as good as it got, and he'd have to accept it.

Gavin sat in the burgundy chair in the corner and picked up his acoustic guitar from the stand. He strummed a few chords, practicing the beginning of one of the songs he planned to play tonight, when the door to his music room opened.

Mason stumbled in, eyes half-closed, hair a mess, their blanket wrapped around his body that was no doubt still naked. "Too early," Mason mumbled. "But I like being close to you. Like listening to you play." And then he fell onto the couch on the other side of the room, curled into a ball and closed his eyes. Most of the time, Mason was more of a morning person than Gavin, but it had been a long night.

Gavin's heart swelled as he took him in, studied the strong, confident man who crawled out of bed just to be in the same room with Gavin as he played. They were so damn lucky to have found each other.

Gavin watched Mason as his fingers danced up and down the fretboard. Watched the blanket move as Mason's chest rose and fell. Watched him scratch the dark scruff on his face before mumbling in his sleep and then changing positions.

Mason's leg rocked to the tune of Gavin's song as he slept, and as crazy as it sounded, he thought his damn heart followed along as well.

He wanted to spend the rest of his life with this man. Yes, he'd known that since he realized he was in love with Mason a long time ago, but taking him in now, watching him and knowing that this man was *his,* he thought maybe it was time to make things a little more official.

What better time was there than now? The holiday season? Gavin didn't want to wait. He wanted to show this man how much he loved him, to ask Mason to belong to him forever.

If he was being honest, he'd admit this was something he'd had in the back of his head for a while.

Gavin's heart sped up and his fingers fumbled on the chords. It was only Mason who ever made that happen to him, but holy shit, he wanted to go out and get a ring. Gavin didn't know why the quiet thought in the back of his mind suddenly became a hurricane force storm in his head. Why this moment, watching Mason sleep after he came in the room just to be close to Gavin kicked him into gear. All he knew was that it was true. He wanted to get down on one knee and ask Mason to marry him. He'd write him a song, that was a given. It didn't give him much time, but he knew he could do it. He felt too strongly about the bossy man.

His fingering messed up again as he played a wrong note.

"You keep screwing up over there. You thinking about me too hard?" Mason's eyes didn't open, his voice scratchy with sleep.

Yes. "Maybe."

"Stop thinking. Just play. I want to listen to you."

Gavin tried to do as Mason said, but he couldn't stop his brain from spinning. The longer he thought about it, the more he realized he really wanted this. Wanted to marry the man who taught him to live. The man who even when they weren't jumping out of planes together, taught him to fly.

-4-

MASON WOKE UP slowly, but kept his eyes closed as he listened to Gavin practice his guitar. He knew exactly what he would see when he opened them—Gavin in the corner, his dark blond hair against his forehead. A wrinkle between his eyes as he concentrated on the music he loved so much.

Today was a big day for Gavin, a big day for Mason, too.

Finally, he let his eyes flutter open and looked over at Gavin. He had his head down. His eyes were probably closed like they so often were when he played. It was like music transported him somewhere else, took him away. Seeing Gavin play was a beautiful sight that Mason felt so fucking honored to experience.

When Gavin missed a note, Mason frowned. He'd missed quite a few this morning. That was unlike him.

"Fuck," Gavin groaned from the other side of the room.

"Are you nervous?" Mason asked. He looked up and their eyes locked.

"Yes, but I don't know why. Not really. I just feel a little on edge." There was something different to the tone of his voice, as though he was hiding something. He had no fucking clue what Gavin could want to hide from him, so he figured he must be reading him wrong.

"Yeah." Mason sat up and ran a hand through his hair. "Yeah, me too."

He watched a smile tease at Gavin's lips. It made Mason smile as well.

"What are you nervous about? I'm the one playing."

Why was he not surprised that Gavin asked him that? Mason

picked up one of the throw pillows from the couch and tossed it at him. "Because I love you, asshole. When you're nervous, I am too." But he was really fucking excited on top of it. He had a surprise for Gavin tonight that he couldn't wait to share with him. If it all worked out, Gavin wouldn't expect it, he wouldn't know what to say, and Mason couldn't wait to see it. Maybe that's another reason he was slightly nervous himself.

"I love you, too. Are you hungry? I need to take a break."

The clock on the wall told Mason it was only nine. Gavin must have gotten up even earlier than he realized. Mason always knew when the bed beside him was empty. He'd felt it the second Gavin left the room and hadn't been far behind to join him. It relaxed him to sleep where Gavin was. The music didn't hurt things either. "I could eat." Mason stood, leaving the blanket wrapped around him. Gavin walked over and pressed a quick kiss to his lips and then the two of them made their way into the kitchen.

They made oatmeal and ate together at the table, making small talk. Gavin told him that Braden had used his time at the cabin to tell Wes he wanted to have a baby. Mason smiled, not surprised. He'd known something was up, though Braden didn't share with him exactly what it was. He still remembered when he first met the man. He'd been attracted to him, tried to flirt with him, but Braden hadn't even noticed. He'd been too wrapped up in Wes even though they hadn't officially been a couple yet.

When they'd had problems, Braden showed up at the bar one night, and all it had taken was one look to see how head over heels in love with him Braden was.

The same way Mason now felt about Gavin.

"You're smiling. What are you over there smiling about?" Gavin asked him.

"Nothing. Just thinking about how everything happens for a reason. How so many little things occur in life to get you on the track to where you're supposed to be."

"Sounds awfully deep." Gavin winked at him.

"What can I say? I'm a deep guy. I'm going to go take a shower. What do you say we get out of here for a while?"

"I should practice..."

That answer didn't surprise him. "Not long, just a little breath of fresh air—cold as hell air, but fresh air all the same." It would be good for him to clear his head before tonight.

Gavin nodded and then Mason headed for the shower. He cleaned up, not taking the time to enjoy the feel of hot water against his skin before getting out and drying off. He wasn't surprised to hear Gavin playing again. The man had his guitar next to him all the time when he was home.

After getting dressed he went to the music room. Gavin didn't stop playing when he came in. Mason knew he would if he asked, but he wanted to let Gavin finish what he was doing. They could leave when Gavin was done, or not at all. Whatever his partner wanted.

Mason headed to the piano in the corner of the room. It was the one he'd gotten for Gavin—one of the best purchases he'd ever made. Gavin loved the damn thing and Mason loved anything that made Gavin happy. Plus, watching him play was sexy as hell.

His mind was running, full, hoping everything worked out well tonight. The music helped. Gavin's music always helped.

With his back to his lover, Mason stood, running his fingers over the keys of the piano, not pressing them, just touching... so he wouldn't disturb Gavin.

He didn't know if tonight was going to work out. The thought was a boulder in his gut, weighing him down. He wanted this to go smoothly. He wanted everything perfect for Gavin tonight.

Mason didn't turn when Gavin's music stopped. He didn't turn as he heard his guy come up behind him. He smiled when Gavin wrapped his arms around him from behind, shoving his hands under Mason's shirt. Without needing direction from Gavin, he lifted his arms so Gavin could pull his shirt over his head…which he did. "I just got dressed and now you're taking my clothes off," he said, dropping his head back on Gavin's shoulder as he kissed Mason's neck.

"Would you rather I stopped?" Gavin asked against his skin.

"Don't stop. I'm telling you right now not to stop. I want you on your knees for me, Music Man."

Mason unbuttoned and unzipped his pants as Gavin kissed his way down Mason's back. His face was smooth as he rubbed his cheek against Mason before running his tongue down Mason's spine. "Yeah, just like that."

He heard Gavin's knees hit the ground. Felt his gentle, musician's hands against his hips before Gavin pushed his jeans down. Mason stepped out of them when they reached his feet, before bending over just enough to give Gavin access to him. "Put your tongue on me."

"My pleasure," Gavin said from behind him, and then he felt it, Gavin's warm wet tongue flick over his tender asshole. Mason groaned, bent forward more, and savored the feel of Gavin's tongue against him.

He fucking loved this, loved being licked and eaten and fucked. He'd been slightly nervous when they'd first gotten together. Before Mason, Gavin typically bottomed but Mason was a bottom through and through. He wanted to be fucked, wanted to tell his lover exactly what to do to him before he was taken, and it turned out Gavin fit that bill perfectly. Slightly submissive, not that they were really a dom and sub, but he liked Mason running the show, and yeah, he was good at giving it to Mason, too. He was good at fucking him the way he needed. "A little more." Mason spread his legs farther apart. "Get me ready for your cock."

"Oh, fuck, I already hurt. Wanna be inside you," Gavin said before he dove back in, licking at Mason in earnest again. He pushed at Mason's hole with his tongue, ran it back and forth over his ring. Mason pushed backward, needing Gavin as close as he could be.

Gavin's nails bit into Mason's ass and spread his cheeks.

"That's it. Show me how much you want me. Get me ready, Gav. Give me your fingers."

He heard Gavin spit, making him shiver. Jesus, he loved hot and dirty sex. They could use lube, but if they did Gavin couldn't eat him, and Mason wasn't willing to give that up right now.

He groaned when Gavin pulled back. His hole clenched, ached to be filled, but a second later, there was the familiar stretching that Mason loved so damn much. He looked over his shoulder, saw Gavin concentrating on his ass just as intensely as he concentrated on his music, as he pushed a spit-slicked finger inside him. "You know me better than that. Give me two."

"Fuck, you are so damn sexy. Whatever you want," Gavin said before leaning forward. He licked at Mason's hole, and sucked his second finger into his mouth.

Mason spread farther, kept looking over his shoulder as his sexy as hell lover concentrated on giving him pleasure.

As Gavin worked a second finger inside, Mason let out a deep breath, relaxed because he had his man inside him the way he loved so fucking much. "Give me your tongue. Hold your fingers still and lick me, then fuck me with your fingers."

Gavin did as he was told, tonguing Mason's tender rim, before pushing his fingers deep, and then pulling them out again. He'd wet his fingers each time he pulled out, twisted them, and then scissored Mason's asshole. "Fuck yes," Mason gritted out as his hands accidentally came down on the keys of the piano.

"I'm the musician, not you," Gavin teased as Mason rocked back, wanting Gavin deeper.

Mason's hard, aching cock twitched against his stomach, and then, "Goddamn," he tensed, pleasure shooting through him in every direction as Gavin rubbed his prostate. His dick leaked, precome dripping down his shaft. "Fuck me. Jesus, I need your cock inside me. Stand up and take me right now."

Mason growled when Gavin pulled his fingers free. Yes, he'd just told him to fuck him but he wanted to be full too, and then Gavin was there, kissing the back of his neck. "I thought you'd never ask."

-5-

GAVIN QUICKLY PULLED his clothes off. His prick ached for Mason, throbbed to be inside the man he loved so much.

It was an urgent desire, as though they were on limited time. As though they couldn't do this every day for the rest of their lives. The need for Mason was always that strong, though, this overpowering want that forever simmered right beneath the surface, waiting to be fulfilled.

Mason didn't move, just kept his standing position partway bent over the piano. He loved fucking standing up and Gavin did as well.

Once he was naked, Gavin opened the piano bench and grabbed the lube inside. They had it stashed not just in their bedroom, but here too. Since he never taught lessons in this room, they figured it was pretty safe.

Gavin ran a hand over the smooth globes of Mason's ass— first the left cheek and then the right one. "I love being inside of you."

"Then fill me up. I'm waiting."

Damn, he was lucky being the man who got to love Mason Alexander every day.

Gavin opened the bottle of lube, squirted some in his hand and then stroked his rock-hard erection.

"Hurry up, Music Man. Fuck me." Mason looked over his shoulder and grinned at Gavin.

He felt that smile deep in his soul. "I'm going, I'm going." After squirting more lube into his hand, Gavin rubbed a wet finger back and forth over Mason's hole, pushing the finger in and then pulled it out again.

"I want your dick, baby. Let me feel you inside of me."

Flames ignited inside Gavin. His cock jerked, pulsed with the need to be exactly where Mason wanted him. He pulled his finger out, wrapped his arms around Mason from behind, and thrust inside him in one fluid motion.

Gavin shuddered, dug his blunt nails into Mason's sides as he went completely still, savoring the feel of the tight, hot cave around him.

"Nothin' like feeling your dick inside me," Mason whispered, before pulling slightly away, and shoving back again.

Gavin called out, fighting off his orgasm already. He slid his arms under Mason's, curved them upward so he could grab Mason's shoulders. He squeezed, fingers digging into Mason's flexing muscles as he held on for dear life while jackhammering inside him.

Each time he slid home, Mason's body hugged him, gripped his cock in a hot, delicious clutch.

Mason groaned each time Gavin thrust. He wrapped his right arm around behind him, clutching Gavin's thigh as he filled him over and over and over.

"Yeah, that's it. Right fucking there. You love me just right." Mason spoke breathlessly, his voice deep and filled with lust. "Bend me over more. I want to feel you on me."

Gavin's cock jerked inside of Mason's tight hole, almost shooting him over the edge and into his orgasm.

He stepped backward, Mason following and then he pushed Mason over so both his hands were now on the piano. Gavin slammed into him again before bending over him, his chest to Mason's back, sliding in and out of him.

"I need your hand on my dick, Gav. Jerk me off and make me come."

He let go of Mason's hip, wrapping his right fist around his partner's hard shaft. He jerked him off while he made love to him, using just the right amount of pressure that he knew Mason loved so much.

"That's it, oh fuck that is so fucking it," Mason groaned out just as his ass clenched around Gavin's dick. He kept jerking him, hot come sliding through his fingers as Mason's ass milked his erection.

Gavin's balls drew tighter, burned and then he let loose, filling his guy as he came, thrust after thrust, until he had nothing left inside him.

They both breathed heavily, neither of them moving. Gavin was still inside him, his hand still slick with Mason's come as he held his softening cock.

"I needed that," Mason told him.

"Me, too. Until you, I never knew it could be so good." He hadn't been a virgin when he met Mason, but Gavin hadn't been the most experienced of men, either. Making love with Mason was like nothing he'd ever felt before. He set Gavin free in more ways than one, and taught him how to enjoy life, every part of it, just by being there and loving him.

"Yeah...yeah, me either." Mason leaned up slightly. Reluctantly, Gavin pulled out of him, and stood up. When he went to grab his clothes, Mason clutched his wrist so that Gavin couldn't move. "You're forgetting something, Music Man. Now's gonna be when you want to kiss me."

Gavin's lips stretched into a smile at that, his pulse kicking up. He loved it when Mason told him that. Leaning forward, he took possession of Mason's mouth just as he was told. Oh yeah, he couldn't wait to tie himself to this man for the rest of his life. He didn't know why he hadn't done it sooner.

-6-

"I T'S TOO BAD we can't jump out of a plane today," Mason told Gavin after they finished cleaning up and getting dressed for the second time that day.

"Or go hiking."

Those two activities had become their thing. From the first time they spent together, when they went skydiving and then hiking, it had become a tradition for them. They went a of couple times a year—sometimes just to feel the freedom it gave, other times to clear their minds, or for the adrenaline rush. He'd skydived before meeting Gavin but it became a completely different sensation after going with him for the first time. He didn't think it was something he could ever do alone again.

"Or," Gavin added, "We can curl up in bed and not leave until we have to."

That sounded pretty fucking incredible to Mason, but he knew it wouldn't work. Gavin would be on edge all day. "You need a new tuning rod, right? How about we make a trip to the music store and pick up a few supplies, grab some lunch, and then get ready for tonight."

Gavin nodded. "Okay, sounds good to me."

So that's what they did. They drove to the music store. What should have taken five minutes took an hour, because that's what happened when you mixed music and Gavin. Mason didn't mind, though. He watched Gavin the way he always did, saw the passion shine from him as he walked through the store admiring the instruments. Once they were done, they visited a small café for lunch.

They both got soup in bread bowls, and coffee. They talked about nothing and everything at the same time, which was how it always went with them. Gavin asked about Isaac, and Alexander's. The family business was thriving with his ex running it, and actually, Isaac and Gavin had somewhat become friends. Not the best, mind you, but they were okay with each other in ways they hadn't been before. Gavin didn't know it, but Mason actually arranged for Isaac to be at Creekside tonight.

When they finished eating they got back into the car to head home.

"I tried to call my mom when you were getting ready this morning. She didn't answer. I know it sounds crazy; it's just a missed phone call, but it worries me. I don't like her being so far away."

Mason's heart rate sped up, his hands becoming sweaty on the wheel. This was a worry that had grown consistently stronger for Gavin the past few months. "It doesn't sound crazy. She's your mom, it's understandable. She's okay, though. Try not to worry." It was different for Gavin than it was for Mason. She was all he had left. She was older, and he one hundred percent agreed with the man, she needed to be closer to them. He'd do anything to make that happen for Gavin because he knew it would relieve some of his stress.

When Gavin didn't answer, Mason pulled off the road and into the parking lot of a small, local park. An oversized Christmas tree stood tall in the middle of it. Off to the side, was a bridge and a creek. "It's not hiking or skydiving, but it's something," he said before opening the door to get out.

They both stepped out of the car, the biting cold making Mason shiver. What the fuck had he been thinking? This was a shitty idea. "I'm going to freeze my balls off and it will be all your fault," he teased Gavin who chuckled.

"We can't have that."

"No, we can't." He nudged Gavin's arm then. "What's on your mind, Music Man?"

Gavin didn't answer for a moment as they walked, snow crunching beneath their feet. They followed the path that led to the bridge.

"I want to spend the rest of my life with you."

Mason's gut clenched at Gavin's words. Not because he didn't want the same damn thing, but it felt really out of the fucking blue. "I want that, too." This had to be an offhand comment. It couldn't mean anything more than that. Not right now.

"It's been a few years now. You and me...we're not going anywhere. You're it for me." Sincerity and love poured out of each and every one of Gavin's words. They vibrated through Mason, echoing the same thing he felt.

"You're not going to do anything crazy right now, are you?"

They stopped in the middle of the quiet bridge, the park empty around them.

"No...but would it be crazy?"

Mason fought to hold back his relieved breath. No, maybe relieved wasn't the right word. Not in the standard sense, because he did want to spend his life with Gavin Davis by his side. "No, not crazy. You just have me concerned right now. First the worries about your mom, and now this. What's going on?" Mason asked him.

Gavin leaned forward, gloved hands on the wood bridge. "Maybe its Wes and Braden's news, and just the fact that I love you so much, but I want us all to be okay. To be happy, and fuck, life is short, ya' know? We just have to be happy."

"And you're not?" Mason asked him.

"No. Fuck no, that's not it. I'm happier than I ever thought I would be. I have things I never thought I would have...I guess, I'm just selfish all of a sudden and I want it all, and I want it now. I waited for years to be happy before I met you. I don't want to wait for anything anymore."

Mason breathed a sigh of relief. "That's not selfish. I love that you feel the need to grab onto life and have the things you want.

You deserve it."

Gavin gave him a small smile. "I don't want it to be like this forever. I want my mom close to me so I can make sure she's okay. I want to be able to call you if I'm running late for work and for her to be completely comfortable and appreciative of you stopping by to check in on her for me. I want her to come to our home. Hell, I'm just going to blame Braden for this, because of him and Wes having another kid, but what if we decide to have kids one day? How would they feel knowing their grandmother didn't one hundred percent support their dads? You're mine, Mason and that's not going to change."

Mason's chest swelled, his heart taking up most of the space there. "No, it's not going to change. You're mine, too." He pulled Gavin into his arms, holding him. He didn't know what that was like, having a parent who still struggled emotionally with who he was. He'd always had his parents' support. When he met his biological family, he'd had theirs as well. "We'll be okay. Your mom and I...it's not as bad as you see it. If you're worried about this for my sake, don't. I have you. I love you, and she loves you. She treats me with respect. She's a hundred times better than she was in the beginning. I know it has to be hard on you, but she loves you, Gav. She'd do anything for you."

"Shit," Gavin pulled back. "You're right. I don't know what the hell is wrong with me."

"Nothing," Mason told him. "You have a big heart. There is absolutely nothing wrong with that."

"Thank you," Gavin winked at him. "And just so you know, regardless of everything else, no matter what happens, you're still mine. Now and forever."

Jesus the man was going to kill him with that forever talk all of a sudden. Mason didn't understand the sudden rush coming from Gavin. If he fucked this up, Mason would kick his ass.

-7-

APPARENTLY THERE WAS something in the air in December.
First it was Braden taking Wes away for the weekend, which led to the couple deciding to try and have a baby. Next came Gavin's decision to propose to Mason, but also his...emotional episode in the park, whatever that had been about.

Everything he'd said to Mason had been true. It did bother him that his mom had to try so hard to accept them. It worried him that she was alone. He wanted her close. He wanted her to love the man he would hopefully be marrying, but he didn't know what made it come out the way it had.

That was all Gavin thought about as they finished their ridiculously cold walk. They went home and he spent part of the day playing, and the rest of it with Mason—and thinking of his mother. He'd called her two more times and didn't get an answer. His gut sank more with each call, even though Mason told him not to worry and that everything was okay.

Her being quiet wasn't unheard of, he reminded himself. She kept busy with her church, but today he felt an unexpected need to speak to her. Likely because of the decision he'd made about Mason.

When the time came, they made the quick drive to Creekside, which didn't help his nerves. Like he told Braden earlier, it's not like he was playing for a crowd of thousands. It was their friends in Blackcreek and nothing more.

Gavin sat in the back office, the door closed and his guitar in his hand. Mason was in the main part of the bar. He knew

Gavin's routine well, knew that he would stay locked in here until he took the small stage to play.

When there was a quiet knock at the door, Gavin's eyes shot up before saying, "Come in."

"How's it going, Rockstar?" Braden asked as he stepped into the office, closed the door and then leaned against it. Gavin rolled his eyes.

"You're a funny man."

"So I've been told. It's part of my charm."

He definitely didn't lack self-confidence. He never had. "I'm doing okay." Gavin paused a moment to think, then decided to just go for it. Who knew, he might need his friend's help to pull off whatever it was he decided to do. "I'm going to ask Mase to marry me. Soon. I don't want to wait." What was the point? Not when it had taken so long to find each other and he knew they both wanted the same thing.

There was a brief moment of shock on Braden's face before he smiled. "No shit? That's fantastic, man. Congrats."

"Thank you. I'm not sure what I'm going to do. I just know...Hell, I just know I want things official. I love him. I don't want to wait." The old Gavin would have. He would have wanted things planned out better. He would have second-guessed himself, even though he knew it was what was right for him, because he'd been scared to live. He hadn't really known *how* to just live his life before Mason. However, from the second Mason talked him into jumping out of a plane with him, when they'd fallen thousands of feet through the air together, flying, part of him knew that the best kind of living would happen with Mason by his side.

He needed to experience life, grab it by the fucking balls and live it.

He could go shopping for a ring while Mason was at work. He wanted to see his mom anyway, so he could make that trip afterward. Once he had the ring and spoke with his family, what else did he need? Just him and Mason. That was all. He could do this. He could plan a quick proposal.

Braden glanced at his phone, then quickly returned his eyes to Gavin. "Good for you. You only live once. I'm glad you see that now."

When they'd dated, Gavin hadn't. He'd still thought he could keep who he was a secret, and be happy just having a job he'd love. Braden tried to show him otherwise, but he hadn't been able to see it. He wasn't able to see it until there was someone in his life he wasn't willing to hide, someone he wasn't willing to live without. "I do."

"Are you nervous about playing tonight? Mason says you always are. You know you're going to do great."

After setting the guitar down, Gavin leaned forward, placing his elbows on the desk. "I'll always be nervous. That's a good thing."

"It is?"

"Yep."

Braden nodded and Gavin could tell his friend knew where he was coming from. "I can't believe you're getting hitched." He playfully shook his head and Gavin laughed.

"Well considering I haven't asked him yet, maybe I won't be. He could say no."

Braden rolled his eyes. "You know better than that. The guy is crazy about you." And Gavin did know better. He knew what Braden said was true. He wasn't sure how he got that lucky, but he had. After Braden glanced at his phone again, he nodded toward the door. "We should get out there."

Gavin's brows furrowed. Mason usually came back to get him before he played, even if it was just to razz him about being nervous, which was his way of wishing Gavin good luck.

He stood, his stomach in familiar knots. "I wonder where Mason is."

"It's really busy. He got hit pretty hard. Looks like everyone in town is excited to see you play tonight."

That made the knots in his stomach tighter. They would be

like that until he started to play, and then the music would overpower everything else. "Let's go, then." Gavin grabbed his guitar and followed Braden out of the room. It was uncharacteristically quiet as he made his way down the hallway. When they made it to the end, Braden stepped out of the way. The second Gavin rounded the corner he saw it.

He saw *him*.

His Mason, kneeling in the middle of the stage, on one knee, a small box in his hand.

Gavin's heart pounded rapidly, each echo of vibration somehow whispering Mason's name. The man he loved. The man who was on one knee right now, with a ring in his hand.

The man who'd beat him to the punch. Somehow, Gavin wasn't surprised. And he also couldn't make himself move. He just wanted to take him in, to capture this moment.

His man gave him a cocky smile, and jerked his head slightly as if to say, *come here.* "Gonna keep me waiting forever, Music Man?" he asked and damned if Gavin didn't smile so big his face hurt. He felt almost animated, one of those bold, happy, singing cartoons that glowed so fucking bright.

He felt Braden's hand come down on his shoulder, and squeeze. Gavin didn't look back at him, just handed Braden his guitar and he started walking toward Mason. He only made it a few steps before he saw one of the tables from the corner of his eye. It was a small, round table, right in front of the stage.

Mason's parents were there, but that wasn't what held his attention. It was the fact that Gavin's mom sat in the chair next to them.

His breath caught. His chest ached in the best way. She looked out of place, unsure as she stared at him...but she was here. She was here for Gavin. She was sitting in Mason's bar right now, her first time in Blackcreek, because she knew that Mason wanted to ask him to marry him.

She was here, offering him her support.

Gavin knew that was all because of Mason.

He waited, looked at her...and then it happened. She gave him a small smile, and then nodded toward Mason as if to tell Gavin to keep going to him.

And so he did. His legs shook as he headed toward Mason, whose eyes were watching him intensely. They shook as he stepped onto the stage, as he walked over to his guy, stopping in front of him.

"I spent weeks trying to come up with some kind of big speech. It's a lot of pressure when you're in love with a guy who writes music. You've written me a fucking song," Mason glanced toward the table where Gavin's mom sat, "Sorry about the language." There were a few quiet laughs, but then Mason started speaking again. "It was driving me crazy trying to figure out what to say. You would have been better at this part than me. All I can say is, marry me, Music Man. Spend your life flyin' with me."

There was absolutely nothing better Mason could have said. "Come here. Of course, I'll marry you." He grabbed Mason, pulling him to his feet, before tugging him into a tight hug. They clutched each other, their bodies as close as they could get. With his mouth next to Mason's hear, he said, "You stole my thunder. I was going to propose to you."

Mason laughed, the shaking in his chest and stomach vibrating through Gavin. "I had a feeling. You scared the shit out of me with all that forever talk all of a sudden. I thought you were going to get to it before me." He pressed a quick kiss to Gavin's lips. "You can propose to me too, if you want, but right now I really want to put my ring on you."

"In a minute," Gavin whispered. "I want to hold you." So he did, right there in the middle of the stage with their friends and family surrounding them, cheering and clapping. He knew without looking that everyone they loved was there to celebrate with them. "My mom is here," he quietly whispered.

"I know." Mason's grip on him tightened.

"Thank you," Gavin told him.

"Nothing to thank me for. Now can I please put my ring on

your finger?"

Gavin let out a loud laugh and pulled back. "Yeah, yeah you can."

Mason opened the box before sliding the black band down his finger. There were more loud claps and cheers in the bar. He looked out into the crowd of people, smiling, wanting to thank them all for being here, wanting to sneak away with Mason to thank him properly, but there was something he needed to do first, someone he needed to see.

"Use the office. I'll keep everyone busy out here." Mason solved his unspoken problem.

He nodded, and then pulled Mason in for a quick kiss. "I love you. I can't wait to spend my life with you."

Mason winked at him. "You're stuck with me now."

There was nowhere else he'd rather be.

People patted Gavin on the back, offering their congratulations as he made his way off the stage. He thanked them all, and no one kept him, obviously knowing he had somewhere to be.

When he reached the round table with his and Mason's family, Mason's mom was the first to her feet. She pulled Gavin into a hug, "Congrats, sweetie. I'm so happy for the two of you. I can't wait to plan a wedding!"

He laughed, not surprised at her words. "Thank you." She'd do a hundred times better of a job at it then he or Mason would.

Mason's dad stayed seated. He still had lasting effects from his stroke, but he shook Gavin's hand, giving Gavin congrats as well.

Isaac only winked at him and smiled. The whole time his mom sat nervously in the chair, looking at the purse on her lap, the floor, anywhere except at him. His gut twisted. His palms were sweaty. He didn't know what to say to his own mother. "Hey, Mom. I'm glad you could make it."

"Thank you." She fiddled with the strap on her purse and all he thought was *fuck it*. Life was too short for this. He held out his hand to her, and she took it. Gavin helped her to her feet and the second she stood, he hugged her with more strength than he ever remembered doing.

"It means the world to me that you're here," he told her.

There was a pause, a quiet cry against his chest and then she whispered. "It shouldn't have taken me so long to come. I...I love you. There's nowhere else I'd rather be."

And just like that, everything was complete in Gavin's world.

-8-

GAVIN WAS TRULY flying tonight. Mason could see it in everything he did. His performance had been incredible. He'd been on fire in the middle of that small stage, singing and playing his heart out with Mason's ring on his finger.

They'd spent most of the night running around like crazy, in between spending time with family and friends.

Both Gavin and Mason watched out for Gavin's mom. Mason could sense her unease in the beginning, but as the evening went on, she'd loosened up. She had enjoyed seeing her son sing. The pride shone out of her and damned if seeing Gavin on top of the world didn't make Mason feel like he was flying too.

Mason watched as Gavin pulled his mother into a hug at the end of the night. "Are you sure you'll be okay?" he asked her.

"Yes, I'll be fine. Mason took care of everything. He was nervous about me driving in the snow so his family picked me up on the way in. He got a room for me tonight, and he said the two of you will drive me home tomorrow."

Yeah, he'd be lying if he didn't admit a burst of pride swelled in his chest. He'd thought of everything to make sure his future mother-in-law was as comfortable as possible.

"Alright." Gavin nodded at her. "Thanks again for coming. Maybe tomorrow you can come over and see the house before we go? I have a beautiful music room."

Mason held his breath, waiting for her to reply, but he didn't have to hold it for long.

"I'd like that, Gavin. I'd like that very much."

They took another moment to say goodbye. Mason's family

was going to take her to the hotel where they'd gotten a room as well, so no one had to drive out of Blackcreek this late. When they were done, Gavin turned to head back for Mason, when his mom spoke, "Mason...thank you for everything you've done to make my Gavin happy."

Mason went still, didn't know what to do as she closed the gap between them...and hugged him. Once her arms wrapped around him, he snapped out of his shock, and returned the hug. "There's nothing I wouldn't do for him," he said looking at Gavin. "It's him who makes me happy."

She chuckled. "I have a feeling it's something you both do for each other." She pulled back and smiled at him, then smiled at Gavin too, before walking over to the car and getting in. He and Gavin stood there watching until the car lights disappeared.

Gavin turned to him, his eyes stormy with so much fucking emotion it took Mason's breath away. "Do you understand the gift you've given me tonight?"

"All I did was have a conversation with her, Gav. You would have done the same thing. It wouldn't have been right without her here tonight." He shrugged. "I wanted her to see how beautiful our life is...how much I really love you." He winked. "That I plan to make an honest man out of you."

Gavin chuckled, but Mason heard more sentiment in the laugh than amusement. "When we were in the office talking, she told me she saw it. She said of course she knew we loved each other, but being here, speaking with your family and seeing our friends, the life we've built, she saw we have a beautiful life, the same as she did with my father. She said she's proud and she knows he would be, too."

Mason realized in this moment, how much Gavin needed that. They were happy. They would always be happy and no matter what had happened with his mom, it wouldn't diminish their happiness...but he needed this as well. Sometimes it didn't matter how old you were or how settled, people still needed love and support from their family, people they loved. Mason himself felt that way. "I'm proud to be your fiancé, Music Man." Fuck, he loved Gavin so much it hurt. "Take me home. I want my new fiancé to fuck me senseless."

Gavin grinned, grabbed his hand and dragged him to their vehicle.

It was a rush to get home, a rush as they stumbled into the house laughing, a rush as they made their way to their room, stripping.

Once there, though, naked at the foot of their bed, looking at each other, that's when everything slowed down.

Mason leaned in, pressing soft kisses to Gavin's pliant lips. He rubbed his face against Gavin's stubble, liking the burn and roughness against his skin. He wrapped his arms around him, hot skin against hot skin as they made out, Mason's hand's sliding down to cup Gavin's ass.

They slowly moved their bodies together, rubbing their rigid erections against each other. He groaned when Gavin's hands found his ass, when a finger traced down the crack of it—up and down, teasing him.

Mason slid his mouth down Gavin's neck, sucking the skin. "Are you trying to make me beg for it? You know I need part of you inside me. Fuck, I'd have you inside me all the time if I could."

Gavin dropped his head back, pushed his finger deeper into Mason's crack. "You wouldn't beg for it, though. You'd just tell me what to do and I'd do it."

Wasn't that the fucking truth?

"So maybe you should get to telling," Gavin added, making Mason laugh.

"Getting so bossy. If my dick wasn't leaking all over the place, I'd make you hold off just for being so impatient." But the truth was, Mason was impatient too. His whole body pulsed with desire, with the need to make love to his future husband.

Mason pulled away, backed up to the bed, and lay on his back, legs spread wide. "Come here and suck my dick. I want at least a finger inside me too."

Gavin stroked his long, thick prick as he came over. He stopped only to grab lube from the drawer, tossing it to the bed, before continuing to pump his cock as he crawled between Mason's legs.

"You are so fucking sexy, all spread out for me. Sometimes it shocks me that you're mine." Gavin ran a hand down Mason's chest, then used one finger to trace a path down Mason's aching dick.

"Always yours."

Gavin lay beside him. He grabbed the bottle of lube, coating a finger. Mason couldn't take his eyes off Gavin as he leaned forward, sucking Mason's cock to the back of his throat at the same time a wet finger pushed past his ring, and inside him. "Fuck yes. That's what I want."

He thrust as Gavin's hot mouth swallowed him down, clenched around the finger fucking him. Everything was suddenly happening too fast. He wanted it to slow down, wanted to make this night last so he said, "Lick me, suck me slow. I want to savor you."

Gavin smiled up at him, mouth full of cock, and damned if it wasn't the most beautiful sight he'd ever seen.

"You mean like this?" Gavin asked before starting at the base of Mason's erection and slowly running his tongue up, all the way to the slit. He continued lapping at him, up and down, tracing every part of Mason's dick.

"Yes…" Mason hissed out. "Just like that. Give me another finger, and then suck my head, nice and slow."

Gavin pushed another finger inside him, twisting and turn-ing, giving Mason just what he loved…being full. He pushed down on Gavin's hand, hungry for more just as Gavin pulled his crown into his mouth with gentle suction.

He watched Mason the whole time, and Mason watched him, looking down as Gavin made love to him with both his fingers and his mouth. It was enough to turn him inside out, to make him overheat, to make pleasure slide down his spine and his balls fill and ache to explode.

Mason threaded his fingers though Gavin's dark-blond hair, gripped him tight as Gavin blew him.

He felt the burn in his sac, felt it tighten and fill more by the second. He pulled Gavin off him, pulled him up so he lay on top of him and fused their mouths together. They kissed, first urgent and hungrily, then slow and seductively. They rubbed off on each other, their pricks hot and ready. He loved the feel of his man on top of him, loved having Gavin inside of him as well. "Fuck me," Mason told him. Gavin growled against his skin and kneeled between his legs, grabbed the lube and slicked it down his shaft. He teased Mason's hole, making him groan out in pleasure, before pushing Mason's legs back farther toward his chest.

"There's nothing I love more than being inside you," Gavin said before leaning over, and slowly pushing inside. Once the head of his cock passed the ring of muscle, the first tease of pleasure Mason sought overtook him. Gavin slid home, making them both cry out.

"Right there." Mason clutched Gavin's ass. "Don't move. Just let me feel you inside me, filling me up."

Gavin did as he said, holding still, his cock nuzzled tight in Mason's ass. "You're my fiancé," Gavin said as he looked down at Mason smiling.

"Yeah, I am."

"I never thought I'd get married, didn't think something like that was in the cards for me."

It was a luxury the gay population hadn't always possessed, but he knew Gavin meant more than that, he meant for himself personally.

"We were waiting for each other. It's in the cards now. Take me."

Gavin immediately pulled almost all the way out before slamming forward again. Each time he pulled out, Mason wanted him back, wanted to be filled the way only Gavin could do for him. They fucked fast, made love slow. They were sweating, their bodies sticking together, but it still wasn't enough. Mason wanted more. "Wanna ride you."

"Oh, fuck," Gavin said and then flipped them, his cock slipping free when he did. Once he got to his back, Mason grabbed his slick, stiff, erection, put it against his hole and sank back down. "Yes. Fuck, I love being inside you," Gavin sighed.

Mason pulled him up so Gavin was sitting. His arms immediately wrapped around Mason as he rode Gavin's dick. Their mouths met again, tongues fucking the same way Gavin's cock took his ass.

Gavin hit him deeper this way, each thrust making him groan out as the fire inside him burned with more and more intensity.

"Jesus, my balls are going to explode. I'm gonna come, Mase."

Mason wrapped a hand around his erection—one, two, three strokes was all it took. Hot, thick come shot from his slit. He felt the heat of Gavin's semen filling him, shooting inside him as he continued to thrust through the orgasm ripping through both of them.

They fell back against the bed, a mass of sweaty bodies and heavy breathing.

"I can't wait to officially make you mine," Gavin said after a few moments. "Love you so fucking much."

Mason smiled down at him. "I love you too, but I'm kind of looking forward to you proposing to me as well. It sounds fun."

They both laughed. He loved nothing more than loving and laughing with this man.

"You have yourself a deal. I want to be on my knees for you."

That's exactly what Mason wanted to hear. "Now's when you're going to want to kiss me," he said, and his fiancé did just that.

COOPER
&
NOAH

-1-

NOAH WOKE UP to a body on top of his. He knew who it was, of course. Knew the feel of every inch of Cooper's body, knew the weight of him, the scent of smoke washed off his skin with the soap they shared. "Bad night?" Noah asked into the darkness. He wasn't sure how he knew, what made him realize that this wasn't just horny Cooper coming home and wanting to get laid. This was hurt Cooper. The one with demons in his past that through his job as a firefighter got dredged to the surface from time to time. Coop loved what he did; it made him feel like he was respecting the memory of his parents, but at times it broke him down.

Noah was lucky as hell that he was the one who got to soothe him.

"Bad night," he confirmed. "Need you."

"You have me," Noah told him. He'd belonged to Cooper Bradshaw ever since he was ten years old. That wasn't about to change. Not now, not ever.

He tangled his hand in Cooper's wet hair, then pushed him down, so their mouths met. His tongue sunk into Coop's mouth, tasting toothpaste. After a bad fire, he often showered at the station, but would sometimes take another shower in their second bathroom when he worked late, so he didn't wake Noah. It was as though he thought he could wash away the memories. Tonight must have been one of those nights. He pulled far enough away to mumble, "You should have woken me first. I would have taken care of you." He would have washed the remaining traces of fire from Cooper's skin. Would have cleaned and kissed and fucked him until he forgot. There wasn't a damn thing he wouldn't do for Cooper and there never had been.

"You're taking care of me right now. Grounding me," Coop told him and then they were kissing again.

There was nothing in the world like being the man Cooper needed. He'd changed his life for Noah. He'd lost his uncle because they loved each other, but still through it all, he somehow needed Noah. It has always been like that between the two of them—from the moment they collided in air for a football at ten years old.

Their mouths moved together in unison, each knowing how the other liked to be kissed. Cooper slowly rotated his hips, dragging his thick, hot, cock along Noah's aching one.

Noah wrapped his arms around Coop, pulling the man against him as tightly as he could, while Cooper took what he needed from Noah's mouth.

When Cooper pulled back, his face moving to Noah's chest, licking and sucking on his nipple piercings, Noah said, "Let me suck you."

Cooper didn't answer right away, laving his tongue back and forth over the piercings he loved so much. Noah had told him from the beginning that men liked it, now he saw firsthand. Finally, he pulled his mouth away and said, "You'd...you'd do that?"

Noah let out a deep laugh. There was his Cooper, easing his way out of the past and back into the present where he belonged. "After all these years you still remember saying that?" he asked, running his hand down Cooper's muscular back to palm his firm ass. He'd asked that before Noah gave him head for the first time. In Cooper's defense, he'd never been with a man before and had felt out of his element.

"I remember it all."

Noah smiled into the darkness. "Yes. I'd so fucking do that," he repeated the same thing he'd said to Cooper that night. "Get up here and straddle me. I want your weight on me when I have your dick down my throat."

Cooper's familiar sarcasm was in his voice when he said, "If you insist."

And then he pulled away, did as Noah said and straddled his chest, his weight on Noah as his cock pressed against Noah's lips. There was nothing like the taste of his man on his tongue.

Noah opened up for him, as Cooper angled his erection down and slid it past Noah's lips. He sucked the head, tonguing the slit, before grabbing Cooper's waist and pulling him deeper to take all the way to the back of his throat.

"Oh, fuck. Yes, Noah. Like that. Damn, I love that mouth of yours."

Noah loved his as well. Not just when he used it on Noah's body either. He loved just listening to Cooper speak. He was funny, charming, and the most honest man Noah had ever known.

He smelled their soap on Cooper's skin. Tasted his pre-come every time Cooper thrust forward, filling his mouth again. Cooper's hands tugged at his hair. His breathing sped up, soft moans echoing through their bedroom.

Noah ran his finger down Cooper's crack, squeezing his ass cheeks as his man filled his mouth over and over again.

Cooper pulled out of his mouth with a pop and Noah went to work on his balls, sucking and licking at the heavy sac. He wanted Cooper's mark all over him, which he knew Coop was okay with. The man was jealous as hell when it came to Noah and he wouldn't have it any other way. He would wear a sign saying he belonged to Cooper Bradshaw if the man wanted him to.

"Jesus, Noah. You feel so damn good. Need you inside me, though."

His dick jerked against his stomach at that, pre-come leaking on his skin. Being inside Cooper was his favorite place to be. "Let me up, baby." He gave Cooper a swat on the ass. "But then don't move. I'm going to take you right here."

Cooper moved to the side, and Noah got out from under him. Noah hit the light beside their bed, wanting to see his beautiful, sexy man as he made love to him.

Cooper smiled at him, but it didn't reach his eyes. Yeah, it had definitely been a bad night for him. Noah would do anything to wipe those memories away for good…but was that something you ever got over? Knowing your parents died in a fire, saying goodbye to your mom as she forced you to flee knowing that she wouldn't make it. He didn't think so. Cooper had him, and he talked to someone about it, but Noah figured those demons didn't ever go away completely.

He'd do anything to shove them aside for as long as he could.

"Grab onto the headboard, baby. I want you right here. Gonna fuck you good until there's nothing left but us."

Noah plucked the bottle of lube from their bedside table. Cooper was still kneeling, legs spread, ass poked out, looking over his shoulder at Noah as he lubed his fingers.

Cooper cried out when Noah pushed two, wet fingers inside his tight hole…and then… "Fuck yes, Noah."

That's what he liked to hear. Noah pushed his fingers in as deep as he could, loving the feel of Cooper's heat surrounding him. He twisted and stretched Cooper, his guy shoving his ass back each time he did.

They liked rough sex, always had. There was nothing like the feel of not having to go easy, but right now he knew that wasn't what Cooper needed. "You are so fucking beautiful." Noah wrapped his other hand around Cooper's body, ran his fingers down his chest before fisting Cooper's dick. "So sexy…so mine."

"Fuck me, Noah," Cooper groaned out. Noah's cock wept but he wasn't ready yet. He still wanted to play.

"I'm getting there, baby. Remember the first time I touched you here?" He thrust his fingers inside Cooper again making another cry rip from his throat.

"Nope," Cooper replied breathlessly and Noah couldn't help but laugh.

"Smart ass."

"I'm serious. I don't remember. Maybe you should remind me." Cooper pushed back again. "Where were we?"

"My workshop…the workshop you gave me." Noah played along with Cooper's game.

"That was sweet of me. Sounds like I'm a good boyfriend."

"The best." Noah's body was lined up behind Cooper's, the fingers of his right hand still in his ass, his left jerking Cooper's prick. "I felt so fucking lucky, and I wanted to thank you properly. Do you remember what happened next?" he asked against Cooper's neck, and the man shuddered, fucking shuddered. He would never get used to getting that kind of response from Cooper.

"No…I think you should remind me." Noah curled his fingers. "Oh fuck, Noah. Right there." A bead of sweat trickled down Cooper's face and Noah licked it, loving the salty taste.

"I bent you over like you are now, only you were standing up. You had your hands on my counter, and then I kneeled behind you, took your pants off and spread your cheeks. I told you how fucking sexy your hole was, waiting for me, just like it is now."

"Then why don't you fuck it?" Cooper asked.

"I am."

"With your dick."

"I'm getting there." He licked a path up the back of Cooper's neck. "That was the first time you let me have my tongue in you. I was fucking gone right then. Though in a lot of ways, I was gone for you before that."

Noah was torturing himself right along with Cooper. His dick hurt. His balls were heavy and full. "I used my tongue…then my finger. Now I get to use more than that, don't I?"

"Yess… Unless you don't get going and I kill you first."

Noah chuckled again. He had Cooper fully in the moment, wanting nothing else other than for Noah to make love to him. The memories that plagued him earlier were gone and Noah knew it.

Noah pulled his fingers out, before lubing up his cock. He ran it up and down Cooper's crack. "What do you want, baby?"

"I want you to fuck me. Hard."

Noah could definitely do that. He put the head of his dick at Coop's entry and thrust in. Heat scorched through him. His balls burned, almost releasing right then and there.

He threaded his fingers through Cooper's on the headboard, pulling out before thrusting in again. Noah took him; each time he pumped in, Cooper's tight channel squeezed like a fist around his cock.

"Finally," Cooper said as Noah slid home again. "Still love it just as much as I did the first time. There's nothing like having you inside me."

There was nothing like being there.

Noah took him hard. The headboard banged against the wall. A picture fell, clattering to the floor, but it didn't slow them down. Cooper met each of his thrusts. Their sweat ran together. Noah looked down, watching his cock slide in and out of Cooper's ass and the burn in his sac kicked up another notch. "It's so beautiful, watching my dick inside of you."

"Wear a camera on your head next time. I want to see."

Laughter fell out of him, the kind that only Cooper could give. When Coop laughed too, Noah felt his hole clench around his prick.

"Wrap your arms around me, Noah. Jerk me off."

Cooper clung to the headboard so tightly, his fingers an un-natural shade of white. Noah did as he asked, encircling Cooper in his arms, his right hand fisting around Cooper's pulsing cock as he began jacking him off. He only managed three yanks before hot, sticky come shot from Cooper's slit, sliding down Noah's fingers.

His asshole automatically tightened around Noah, making his balls release, his own come jetting out of him and inside of Cooper. He kept thrusting until he didn't have anything else inside him anymore, but he didn't move. He clung to Coop's sweat-slick body until Cooper knew everything would be okay.

-2-

"I NEEDED THAT." Cooper still knelt on the bed, holding the headboard. Noah hugged to him from behind, their bodies molded together, and he knew Noah wouldn't let go until Coop let him know it was okay.

"Just like I need to be the one to give it to you."

Death from a fire always took a lot out of him. It had the power to bring back the memories of losing his own parents, memories Cooper wasn't sure he would ever forget.

He was okay. The past didn't grab ahold of him nearly as much as it used to—only after situations like tonight, and he knew he always had Noah to bring him back to Earth again. "My buddy has a camera he wears on his helmet when he rides motocross. Maybe we can get you one of those. You can wear a headband and attach it so I see everything from your angle when we're fucking."

Noah didn't laugh, probably because he knew Cooper was trying to be funny instead of talking about anything serious. "Fine, be that way. Next time I'll just jerk off in the shower."

"No you won't," Noah said against his skin. "I won't let you out of this bed, even to go to work."

Staying in their bed didn't sound like such a bad thing to Cooper...but then, they did have a special occasion coming up. Cooper and Noah's Winter Wonderland was only a couple days away and Coop couldn't wait. He had more in store for this party than even Noah knew. "The only reason I'm not arguing about the whole you keeping me in bed thing is because I have a party to plan. Come on, lie down with me, Noah."

They pulled away only enough so that they could lie down. Noah wrapped an arm around him and Coop put his head on Noah's chest. He rasped his thumb back and forth over one of the piercings there, reveling in the feel of him. Every day he was thankful that Noah Jameson came back into his life, turned it upside down and completed it. "It was an elderly gentleman. He lived alone. We couldn't get him out in time. He was likely gone by the time we got there."

Noah squeezed him tighter and placed a kiss on the top of his head. "I'm sorry, baby."

"Yeah…yeah, me too."

"You save a lot of lives, Cooper. You save people's loved ones, their homes, their pets. You have to remember the good."

And Cooper did. Hell, he still kept in touch with the kid he helped when he got hurt a few years back—Billy. He was a young man now, a teenager, going to school dances and playing sports all because Cooper had saved him. He knew that loss was part of the job. It wasn't always easy to deal with, but there was a lot of fucking beauty in it too.

"It's so easy for you to make me feel better. Just being with you." Back and forth, he still let his thumb tease Noah's nipple piercing.

"That's what I'm here for, the same way you're for me. Always, Coop. You know that. Even from when we were kids. You are the only one in my life who has always made everything better." That's what they'd always done for each other. Somehow from the second they met, there was something special between them that would never go away.

"It's probably because I'm so damn sexy. Or my blow job ability. I've only been sucking dick for a few years and I could probably be some kind of world champion at it."

Noah's laugh vibrated from his chest and into Cooper's. There was the laughter he wanted.

"What am I going to do with you?" Noah asked.

"Just love me," he replied. "Love me and say yes to whatever I want. Always say yes, no matter how crazy you think I am." This he was serious about. Cooper got some wild ideas, probably some stupid ones and annoying ones, but figured that didn't matter as long as Noah went along with them.

"You know I've never been able to say no to you."

Cooper smiled as Noah turned off the light. Yeah, he did know that. He was so fucking lucky.

COOPER SPENT HIS morning shopping. It definitely wasn't his favorite thing to do, but he had a lot to do to get ready for the party. When Noah agreed to have it, it was with the understanding that Cooper would do most of the work. Of course he knew that Noah would help if he needed, but this was Cooper's show and he would run it. Hell, he hadn't let anyone in on what he had in store for the night, and he liked it that way. This was all him and he couldn't wait for all to be revealed.

It was five minutes after one that afternoon when he pulled into the parking lot of Creekside. Noah was working at his store today, which was incredibly busy this time of year. People loved his handcrafted furniture, especially for the holidays. Still, he'd managed to carve out some time for lunch and they decided to meet here.

Cooper grabbed the bag from the passenger seat (the others he'd already hidden away) and made his way into the bar. Mason was behind the counter; his new fiancé, Gavin, sat on Noah's left, and another man Cooper didn't know sat to Noah's right.

Noah said something and then all four men laughed, the dude he didn't know putting a hand on Noah's shoulder. He leaned closer, showing Noah a piece of paper, his hand still touching. Cooper didn't move as they chatted over whatever was on the paper, and the motherfucker still didn't move his hand off Noah.

He'd never been a jealous man. He'd never felt any kind of

jealousy until Noah walked back into his life. Now? Now he felt it over the most ridiculous things. He knew Noah was his. He trusted him, but stemming back to walking into the bar years ago and seeing Noah with Wes, irrational jealousy always burned through him when it came to Noah and any other man.

And seriously? Why the fuck was he still touching Noah? *You're an idiot, chill out,* he told himself, but Cooper ignored any sense of reason and stalked over to Noah knowing the whole time he was being crazy.

He stepped right up behind them, grabbed the man's hand, and took it off Noah's shoulder. Noah, Gavin, Mason, and Hands all froze. Slowly, Noah started to turn his way when loud laughter rang in his ear. They were laughing at him—Noah, Gavin and Mason were all three laughing at him.

"I don't see what's so funny." Cooper crossed his arms, pouting.

"Did I miss something?" Hands asked, and it only made the other three men laugh harder. Yep, he was going to kill them. Kill them all.

"Shut up."

Yes, they all knew Cooper was irrationally jealous when it came to anyone and Noah. So sue him.

"Why can't Braden be here right now?" Gavin asked. "How could he miss this?"

"Shut up," Cooper said again feeling sillier by the second.

"I'm assuming there's a private joke here that I'm not in on," Hands said. "And I'm also assuming this is your partner that you never stop speaking about, Noah?"

Noah finally stopped laughing enough so he could say, "Yes," before he wrapped an arm around Cooper's waist and pulled him close. "Jake, this is Cooper Bradshaw; Coop, this is Jake. Remember I told you about him? He and his husband commissioned a crib that I'm making for their baby boy who will be here next year."

Oh...okay. Now he felt a little stupid. But still, why did he need to touch Noah? "Hey, man. Nice to meet you." Cooper held out his hand and the guy shook it.

"You too." And then he looked at Noah. "Anyway, this looks great. I'll show it to Chad and we'll call you. I should get back to work." Jake stood, said his goodbyes and left.

"*Cooper*," Noah said the second Jake was gone.

"*Noah*," Coop replied.

"Seriously?"

"He was touching you—and not just a quick touch either. I didn't know who he was. I just walked in and saw his hand on you. I had flashbacks to that night at the bar with Wes. You should be consoling me right now. It felt tragic."

The three men laughed at Cooper again, and yeah, he had to fight to hold back his own laugh as well. Deciding to change the subject, he sat on Jake's empty stool and tossed the bag to Noah. "I got you something."

"You're forgiven," Noah said, before opening the bag and pulling out the gift. He unfolded the sweater. It was bright green, decorated with a strand of oversized Christmas lights on it. It was ugly as hell. "Maybe you're not forgiven. What the hell is this?"

"It's a sweater," he replied.

"An ugly sweater," Mason added.

"Exactly! It's the theme of Cooper and Noah's Winter Wonderland. This year it's ugly sweaters, next year it's sexy Santa. I have one too. We're going to match."

It was as if the whole bar quieted before Noah's voice broke through, "No. Hell no. I'm not wearing this thing."

"Yes, you are."

"No, I'm not."

"Noah!"

"Cooper!"

And then Noah looked him in the eyes and Cooper said, "Please?"

He knew right then and there that Noah would say yes. "I hate you," Noah told him.

"I love you." Cooper smiled. Jesus, he fucking loved his man.

"You are so screwed!" Mason said, laughing, Gavin doing the same from the other side of Noah.

"I don't know what the two of you are laughing about. You have to wear one too. They're waiting at the house for you. Everyone else knows, but I didn't tell you guys or Wes and Braden because I knew one of you would let it slip. You change at the door. No sweater, no Wonderland, and I'm telling you, this party is something you don't want to miss." Because it was more than just a party, only none of them knew it except for Cooper.

-3-

IT WAS DARK when Noah got home that night, carrying his ugly sweater in the same bag that Coop had given it to him in. What in the hell was he going to do with Cooper? He was the only person Noah knew who would throw an ugly sweater Christmas party. Actually, that was a lie; he was pretty sure Braden would. He wouldn't be surprised if it was Braden's idea. The two of them were nothing but trouble when they were together.

"So we really have to wear these things?" Noah asked him as he made his way into the living room. The room was almost completely decorated in things that Noah had made. They'd remodeled their home together. Noah had furnished it. It was the only real home Noah had ever had—one that he knew he would never have to leave.

"Yes, we really have to wear them. I picked up Chinese for dinner. It's on the kitchen counter."

"Couldn't we go with a Sexy Santa theme first?"

Coop cocked a brow at him. "Do you have a fetish I don't know about?"

Noah rolled his eyes. "Oh yeah, baby. He does it for me." He made a quick turn for the kitchen, grabbed his food and then joined Cooper on the couch. This was his favorite part of life, the everyday living. Coming home to each other every night—no fighting, no picking up and leaving. They were settled. Comfortable. It was perfect. "So an ugly sweater party, huh?"

Cooper smiled at him. "Cooper and Noah's Winter Wonderland—Ugly Sweater Edition."

Noah couldn't hold back his laugh. Jesus, he loved this crazy man.

"So what do I have to do to help you get ready for this thing? Shop's closed until after Christmas."

Cooper shrugged. "Tomorrow you're going to have to spend the day with me, that's what I need you to do. We'll decorate, and take care of things around the house. Christmas Eve we'll pick up the food. I don't want you to do anything else that day other than to follow my lead. I'll take care of everything."

"Follow your lead, huh? That's a scary thought."

Cooper just nudged him and turned back to the TV. They watched ESPN while Noah ate his dinner. When he finished he put the plate away and went back into the living room with his partner. "You know we have to watch it, right?"

Cooper's blue eyes held him, all emotion. "Now's as good a time as any." He nodded for Noah to come back to him as he picked up the remote, went to the movies.

A Christmas Story immediately started to play as Noah took his spot at the end of the couch. Coop lay down and put his head in his lap. Noah's hand went to his hair, playing with the dark-blond strands.

"Thank you for starting this tradition."

Noah smiled down at him. "It wasn't me who started it, baby." Their first Christmas together Cooper had told him that he and his parents used to watch *A Christmas Story* together every year, and so they'd done it, then again the year after that and so on. So no, it wasn't Noah who started it. His parents had with Coop and then Cooper shared that tradition with Noah.

"I think they'd like this…that we watch this every year."

It didn't matter that they knew the movie by heart. It didn't matter that they were men in their thirties watching a movie about a kid who wanted a bb gun. It was their thing—one of them at least, and a way to keep Cooper's parents a part of their lives. "I know they would." He wished like hell he could have met the people who brought this man into the world. They had to be incredible.

They watched it like the first time—laughing at Ralphie in his bunny suit, tongues stuck to poles, and tacky leg lamps.

Coop didn't move from his spot, head in Noah's lap, and Noah didn't take his hand out of Coop's hair, stroking it for nearly two hours.

When the movie ended, they made their way upstairs for the night. They showered together and Noah took care of Cooper the way he would have the night before. He washed him, kissed him, sucked him till he came in three long spurts down the back of his throat, before Cooper did the same for him.

They got out, dried off and then naked, made their way to bed.

They lay in the dark a few minutes, Cooper wrapped around him when he asked Noah "You trust me, right?"

Noah felt his forehead wrinkle at the question. "Who are you and what did you do with Cooper? I'm not going to answer that question because it's ridiculous, and even if there was a chance that I could possibly say no, you'd bulldoze me over until I folded and did trust you."

"You know you just answered my question, right?" Cooper chuckled.

Noah felt a foreign twist in his gut. He didn't like questions like that coming from Cooper. That wasn't how they worked. "I'm worried that you feel like you had to ask it. What's going on with you?"

Coop rolled over on top of him, settling between Noah's legs. His weight was heavy against Noah, just the way he liked it—all Cooper's hot hardness covering him. "Nothing is going on with me. You know how I am. I was fishing for you to tell me how fucking incredible I am. *Of course I trust you, Cooper. You're the sexiest man in the world, Cooper. I want to spend every day of the rest of my life in bed with you, Cooper.* Thanks for fucking up my fantasy."

Noah let out a loud laugh just as he felt Cooper's tongue swirl over his nipple. "Of course I trust you, Cooper." He tilted Coop's head and kissed him. "You're the sexiest man in the world, Cooper." Another kiss. "I will spend every day of the rest of my life with you, in bed or out of it, Cooper." He pushed his tongue past Coop's lips, tasted him before pulling back. "How was that? Good enough?"

"I think I'm going to need a little more convincing."

-4-

"NOAH! GET YOUR ass in here! I made eggs Goddamn it! That's like a fucking miracle."

"Oh is it?" Noah stepped into the kitchen wearing a pair of sweats and a t-shirt. Coop should have turned up the heat so they didn't have to wear as many clothes. He liked it much better when they were naked.

"Yeah."

As Cooper went to grab Noah a plate, Noah told him, "Sit down," and Cooper instantly did. He liked bossy Noah, which was a shock in the beginning, but now there was no surprise that it got him hard.

"You going to serve me?" Cooper asked him.

"I am. You cooked, I'll do this." He plucked two plates from the cabinet before putting a mound of eggs on each. Cooper added chopped onions and bell peppers into them and then topped them with cheese.

Noah set the first plate in front of Cooper and then took the other one and put it at his spot. He made them both cups of coffee before joining Cooper at the table. "They started out as omelets but I fucked them up."

"Tastes the same to me," Noah told him before taking a bite. Cooper wasn't sure why, but the memory of the first time they sat in this kitchen together slammed into him so strong it almost stole his breath.

"In some ways it's almost like it was yesterday."

"When you hit me with your truck?" Noah winked.

"When I rolled into you with my truck. Jesus, you were such

a baby about it."

"You hit me with a fucking truck, Cooper!"

"Didn't we just go over this? I bumped you, but yes, that's what I meant. I hadn't seen you in seventeen years and suddenly there you were, sitting at my table with me. It made no fucking sense, but I had this strange feeling of peace in that moment. It wasn't something I'd realized I was missing until I felt it, sitting there with you." It had and would always be that way with Noah. Maybe it didn't make sense or maybe it made the best kind of sense, but all he knew was Noah always felt different. Noah could always give Cooper something that no one else could.

"Yeah…yeah, I felt it too. Though, I always knew something was missing from my life when they took me away from you."

Cooper mock-rolled his eyes. "Always trying to show me up." He took a bite, then a drink before speaking again. "You rocked my fucking world when you sat there and told me you were gay."

Noah nodded. "I thought it was going to make me lose you after just getting you back, even though it was only friendship at the time."

It threw him for a loop that was for sure.

"I should have known better. I knew you, even though we hadn't seen each other since we were kids, I knew you. Knew what kind of man you were. You wouldn't have walked away because of that. The rest was a surprise though…the jealousy with Wes. Coming home the next day and sitting in this same kitchen when you asked me to touch you. So fucking brave. You've always been the bravest person I know."

Noah always said that to him, but for Coop it was the other way around. Maybe that was part of the reason they worked so well, because of what they were to each other despite everything else.

Cooper was counting on that fact for tomorrow… The fact that they knew each other so well, trusted each other so much and loved each other more than anything. "Sometimes it's hard being this good. You didn't have much choice except to fall in love with me."

Noah gave Cooper a smile that made his chest swell. "No, really I didn't. I didn't know what love looked like before you."

"It looks like you." He said and then glanced at his plate to take another bite. There had to be something in the air in Blackcreek this month. It seemed Cooper and his friends were all turning into big saps.

He couldn't find it in himself to want anything different.

They finished eating before rinsing off their dishes and heading into the living room to begin decorating. "Where do you want me?" Noah asked. It was obvious his lover planned on letting Cooper run this show, which was exactly what he wanted.

But… "That's a loaded question."

"No fucking." Noah shook his head. "We have Noah and Cooper's Winter Wonderland to plan."

"Cooper and Noah's."

"Whatever."

Cooper brought out the bags of decorations and they set out "winterizing" their house.

They strung white lights across the ceiling and around the large sliding glass door in the living room that lead out back. Their eight-foot tree was in the corner of the room along the same wall as the glass door.

Cooper handed Noah's white candles and he set them on every table that Cooper instructed him to. He used green garland, twisted sparingly with silver and made to look like wreaths, on the mantel and the six-foot long table behind the couch. When Cooper pulled out green and silver wreath centerpieces with three candles staggering in height to go in the center of them, Noah's dark brows knitted together. "Aren't you fancy all of a sudden? You really went all out."

Cooper just gave him a simple nod. "I did. It's our first holiday party. It's going to be the best damn party Blackcreek has ever seen."

"I have no doubt about that." Noah winked at him as they

finished setting up. He had a few things hidden in the spare room, but Noah never went in there so Cooper was confident that they would stay hidden.

When they were finished, Noah asked, "Anything else?"

Yes... but nothing you can know about... "Nope. We're good. I'm going to head out for a bit, though. I want to run by the firehouse and take care of a few errands. Do you want me to grab dinner?" he asked.

Noah nodded. "Yeah. Grab anything. I'm easy."

"Yes, you are." Cooper grinned at him and then pulled Noah closer.

"Only when it comes to you." Noah's thumb brushed over Coop's forehead. "There's nothing I wouldn't give you, Cooper Bradshaw."

There wasn't a sliver of doubt in Coop's head that it was true. Noah wouldn't deny him anything, and Cooper wanted to give him everything. "Ooh, I like the sound of that. Want to role-play tonight? You can be my sex slave and I'll be your kinky master."

"Is that really a question?" Noah asked.

"Nope." Because who wouldn't want to play kinky sex games? "Okay, see you soon."

"I'll be out in my workshop. I need to work on Jake's piece. I'm sure I'll hear the truck when you get home."

Cooper growled at the mention of the handsy man, but Noah ignored him. "I won't stay out there long after you get home."

"You better not." He winked at Noah and then pressed one last kiss to his lips. Cooper stepped into his boots, grabbed his coat, hat and gloves and then headed out the door.

He had a lot to do before tomorrow.

-5-

NOAH WAITED UNTIL Cooper left before making his way to his shop—the shop Cooper had given him. After unlocking the door, he turned on the heat to take the chill out. The place was drafty. They'd fixed it up, and had quite a bit of electric work done, but it was still old and didn't hold heat the way it should.

Once he got to work, he'd warm up quickly. Noah made sure to lock the door behind him in case he didn't hear Coop get home. He wasn't working on Jake's piece. He was working on their bed, the new bed he was making as a surprise for Coop.

It had taken him months. There was more detail work in it than anything Noah had ever done. His fingers and hands ached every time he worked on it, as he carved the N and C on the headboard. As he perfected every detail etched into the wood displaying memories of their life together.

He wasn't sure he could bring his vision to life at first. How would he add so many pieces of their history on one object and make it work? But he found a way—the footballs carved at the top of the four posts, the hand on a shoulder in the footboard for those times when they were kids and he'd wake up with his hand on Cooper's shoulder or Coop's hand on his. So many fucking memories giving Noah the kind of life he never thought he'd have.

Showing him what love is.

All because of one man.

The man who was going to make him wear a damn ugly sweater at a party he dubbed Cooper and Noah's Winter Wonderland.

Noah chuckled. Christ, he loved Coop.

Noah set up all of his supplies and then got to work while he had the time. He didn't figure Cooper would be gone too long and he wanted to finish the final touches today, since tomorrow they'd be in Wonderland.

It took Noah a good two hours to finish. It surprised him that Cooper wasn't home yet, but then you never really knew with Cooper. He could still be down at the firehouse shooting the shit with the guys—especially if Braden worked today. The two men were alike in so many ways. Half the time he and Wes didn't know what to do with them, but he knew Wes liked that just as much as Noah did.

And hell…that might be the answer to one of his problems right there. He'd worried about getting the bed set up in the house, figuring that he'd have to show Cooper his gift out here, and then make the man help him carry it inside.

He pulled his phone out of his pocket and dialed Braden.

"Hello?" he answered.

"Hey. Are you at work today?"

"No. I'm meeting your boyfriend down there in about twenty minutes, though. We have some scheduling stuff to work out. Why? What's up?"

Jackpot. "Can you keep him busy for an hour for me? It shouldn't be too hard." It was Braden and Cooper they were talking about for fuck's sake. Both of the men could talk anyone's ear off. "Then call me when he leaves so I know how much time I have?"

"Yeah, sure, no problem."

They said a quick goodbye and then Noah made phone calls to both Wes and Gavin. They both agreed to rush over and help him get set up.

Noah rushed into the house and quickly began taking their bed apart. His friends showed up a few minutes later, and between the three of them, it took no time to get the old bed taken apart and carried down to Noah's shop.

He led them around the corner where the new piece was. It was large—solid—"Wow. That's incredible, Noah," Wes cut off his thoughts.

He watched as Wes ran his hand down the thick oak. Noah knew it really was. He was more proud of this bed than anything else he'd ever made.

"Thank you."

"If everything works out with the surrogacy, Braden and I would love for you to furnish the baby's room."

Baby. It was still a bit of a shock that they were going to try and have another child, though he wasn't sure why. They were great parents to Jessie, but a baby was a whole different story: midnight feedings and diapers. They thrived on fatherhood, and though Noah knew something like that wasn't in the cards for him and Cooper, he could see how happy making a family made Braden and Wes. His friend had come a long way from the man he'd met and tried to pick up one night. "I'd be honored to," Noah told him.

"Cooper will love it," Gavin added and Noah thanked him.

"Okay, let's get this going. I'm sure Braden won't have any problem keeping him, but Coop likes to surprise me sometimes and do the complete opposite of what I think."

They went for the headboard first. Noah knew it was huge. They had a king sized bed and the headboard was solid, which is why he wasn't surprised when Gavin said, "Holy shit. How much does this thing weigh?"

"Don't know. All I can say is with me and Coop sleeping in it, we need something sturdy." He winked at Gavin and all three men laughed.

It didn't take them long to haul everything into the house and put the bed together, but they were sweaty and tired by the end. Just as they finished, Noah got a text. "Okay, Braden said he's leaving. You guys can head out. I'll handle the rest." He only needed to put the box spring and mattress on. "I appreciate all the help."

"Is he serious about this ugly sweater thing?" Gavin asked and Noah just looked at him. "You're right. No shit. This is Cooper we're talking about."

They said their goodbyes and the men let themselves out. Noah finished with the bed, and was putting fresh linens on just as he heard the familiar rumble of Cooper's truck in the driveway. Nerves teased him, not heavy or overwhelming, but there nonetheless. He wasn't sure why. He had nothing to be nervous about. This was Cooper. Still, Noah put his heart into this gift and he wanted Coop to love it as much as he did.

Noah didn't move, didn't head downstairs, as he heard the truck door open and close, then the house door do the same.

"Noah? You in here?"

"Yep! Upstairs," he called back to Cooper.

Footsteps sounded on the stairs, down the hall, around the corner to their room, "Sorry it took so long, I—holy shit, Noah."

Cooper walked into the room, his eyes on the bed. Noah's heart was in his throat as he watched Cooper trace one of the footballs with his finger, the tents from their childhood campouts, the hands on the shoulders, Cooper's truck that had hit him, all engraved into the footboard.

There was more too, and he just watched, held his breath as Cooper traced every inch of his hard work, every inch of what Noah put into their bed. To some people it might be too much, a mishmash of too many things, but for Noah, this was their life together.

And then Cooper stopped, looked over at Noah with more intensity than Noah had ever seen. "Jesus, Noah. This is us. You told our whole life story on this bed."

"Our story till now." Because he knew they had a whole lot more to tell. A lifetime. "Merry Christmas Eve, eve." Noah smiled, but Cooper still didn't move, just looked at him.

"It's the most incredible thing I've ever seen," Cooper told him.

"So is our life."

Cooper didn't speak, he just took off his clothes and climbed into bed. Noah did the same and joined him, and it was where they stayed the rest of the day.

-6-

COOPER WAS NERVOUS as hell.

So many things could go wrong today. Too many things to count, so he tried not to think about them. Usually, he didn't worry much. He went with the flow and forged ahead and while he tried to do that now, worry still plagued him.

This was huge. This could fail. It could be the wrong thing to do.

Or it could be beautiful.

The house was full of people wearing ugly sweaters just the way he wanted it to be. His aunt Autumn was here, but not Vernon. They agreed to disagree years ago and that would never change. He'd thought for a while the man would come around, but he couldn't, and Cooper wasn't okay with anyone who didn't accept Noah. He guessed that happened sometimes in life. Everything couldn't always be perfect.

They were pretty damn close, though.

Wes, Braden and Jessie, along with Wes's sister and her family milled around the house, laughing and talking in their hideous sweaters. Gavin and Mason, friends from work, the bar, customers of Noah's, they were all here.

Holiday music played in the background. People ate and drank. He and Noah spent the morning picking up food and putting the final touches on the house.

Now he waited.

"Why are you hanging out over here in the corner?" Noah stepped up beside him and kissed his head. "I like that our sweaters match. I'll plug my light strand into yours later."

He laughed at Noah's corny joke. "That was really fucking bad, Noah."

"Sorry. I'm not as funny as you."

When a knock came at the door, he and Noah walked over. It was Billy and his family. He was a young teenager now. He'd grown about two feet since that day a few years ago when Cooper had found him in his burning home.

"Oh, hey look! I have lights on my sweater too," Billy told him, and Cooper ruffled his hair, even though the kid was too old for it.

"You have good taste." He said his hellos to the family who then made their way into the house.

Cooper tried to make himself relax, to have fun, but the longer the party went on, the more nerves shot through him.

He could see that Noah knew something was up. He kept his eyes on Cooper the whole night, his forehead wrinkled as though he was trying to figure Cooper out. He had to admit, that did make him smile. Noah didn't have a clue, and that took some of the edge off.

He knew Noah. Noah knew him. Everything would be just fine.

Cooper glanced at his watch and realized he was a few minutes late. The knots returned to his gut as he made his way over to Noah. This had been the hard part—deciding how to go about this. If he should just do it with no warning, or not.

He'd decided to warn Noah. There wasn't a part of him that wasn't confident Noah loved him more than anything, but knowing Noah's past he knew Noah would need a minute.

It was almost like everyone knew what was happening. The room seemed to grow quiet but Cooper knew it was in his head. People parted as he made his way to Noah, who stared at him the whole time.

"I need you to come with me for a minute," he said in Noah's ear. He locked their fingers together and led Noah upstairs. To their room. To stand at the foot of Noah's creation while he laid himself bare.

"What's going on with you, baby? I'm worried. What's wrong?" Noah asked as he shut the door behind him.

"Nothing is wrong." He grabbed both of Noah's hands. His palms sweating. Noah's eyes darkened as he waited for Coop to speak. "Jesus, I love you. I spent every second of my life when we weren't together on hold, waiting for you."

Noah smiled a sexy fucking smile that sent heat zipping through Coop's body.

"I love you, too. I'm going to kick your ass, Cooper. Are you about to do what I think you're going to do?" Noah asked him.

"Nope." He shook his head. He knew Noah would assume he was proposing. Not Cooper, though. Go big or go home. He planned to go big. "In about ten minutes, Autumn is going to start lighting candles, then ushering people to seats. After that she'll change the music and stand under those lights we hung right in front of the sliding glass door, and she's going to wait for us. When we get there, she's going to marry us, Noah Jameson. She's going to legally make you mine."

He saw the shock in Noah's widened eyes, the confusion, the fear, and yeah, the desire, too.

Cooper couldn't wait to make Noah officially his.

-7-

"TEN MINUTES?" WAS the first thing to come out of Noah's mouth. He was supposed to go downstairs and marry Cooper in ten fucking minutes?

He felt himself tense slightly, knew Coop could probably see the confusion on his face and knew the man would understand why.

"We're not them, baby." It wasn't often that Coop used names like that for Noah, but when he did, it was always because he was serious.

"I know." And he did. "I would be lying if I didn't admit that part of it scares me. They're what I know. Their marriage…hell, it wasn't even a real marriage. I have to believe it wasn't always like that for my parents; that thought is in the back of my mind. But then," he rubbed his thumb over Cooper's strong hand. Coop was different. They were different. They loved each other more than anything. Cooper was his soul mate. "We're not them," he confirmed again before standing straighter, confident. Sure. "Ten minutes?"

Cooper laughed and just the sound of it eased some of the tension from Noah's muscles. "How?" Noah asked.

"I asked Autumn to get ordained. I told her I wanted to marry you. I don't know why it feels right to have her do it."

Because she was the only family Cooper had left other than Noah. His parents were gone and his uncle was a homophobe who happened to sleep with Noah's mom years ago. Jesus, that was a fucked up situation. "We always said we didn't need that piece of paper. That we know who we are."

"And we do." Cooper nodded. "We do know who we are and we don't *need* that piece of paper."

They both respected the hell out of anyone who went that route—marriage and kids, but they'd never really seen it in the cards for themselves. Hell, Noah wasn't sure Cooper could handle sharing him with anyone, even if it was a child. They didn't need an official marriage to confirm who they were to each other. They had history and a whole lot of love as their confirmation. He always thought that was all they needed.

"We do know who we are and we don't need that piece of paper. That doesn't mean we can't change our minds, though. It doesn't mean we can't want it. You're mine, Noah. You will always be mine and I want everyone to know you belong to me. I don't want anyone to be able to keep us apart again."

Noah's chest squeezed at that. It had been the worst feeling in the world for the hospital to be able to keep him away from Cooper.

"Look at this, Noah. Look at the fucking bed you made me. Look at our story. Look at our life. We can add this to it next. I want to be your husband in every possible way—in our hearts *and* on that damned piece of paper."

Noah did as Cooper said. He looked at the carvings in the wood; he looked at their story and the longer he did, the more his chest swelled.

He wanted that, too. He wanted to cement the fact that Cooper was his. He wanted to walk down the stairs and marry him at a surprise wedding that only Cooper would come up with. "Are you really throwing us an ugly sweater wedding?"

Coop smiled. "I am."

And in a way it was so fucking them. They were both simple men. They didn't need the long months of planning or to spend all the money. They didn't need people to buy them gifts or to make a big deal out of things, and because they'd come here thinking this was only a holiday party, that's exactly what Cooper was giving him.

And it was perfect.

Until this moment, Noah didn't know how badly he wanted to officially tie himself to this man.

He returned Cooper's smile. "I'm liking the sound of Noah Bradshaw. It has a nice ring to it."

"Really?" Cooper cocked a brow. "I kind of like Cooper Jameson."

"Nope." Noah shook his head. "We should have your parents' last name. That's important to me." They'd given their lives wanting nothing more than for Cooper to live his life, to be happy, and in that sacrifice, they gave Noah his heart.

It was then that the music changed downstairs. Soft guitar music floated up the stairs, and Noah thought that was perfect. They weren't the traditional kind of couple, so traditional wedding music wouldn't work for them.

"I can't believe we're getting married in bright green sweaters with ugly Christmas lights on them."

Cooper leaned forward and pressed his lips to Noah's. "Yes you can and you fucking love it. Now can we please go downstairs and put a ring on it so I have the right to break anyone's hand who touches you?"

Maybe it was wrong, but he loved Jealous Cooper. "You already had that right, baby. Now come downstairs and marry me."

Cooper nodded and Noah didn't let go of his hand as they walked downstairs. He held tight as they made their way through the clearing in the house. Red flames danced on white candles all through the house. Clear lights twinkled around the living room, the main lights were dimmed so they almost looked like little stars in the evening sky.

He smiled at Gavin and Mason as they passed. Then Braden, and finally Wes, who in a lot of ways, was his best friend other than Cooper. Wes gave him a small nod. He said so much in that one action. He was happy for them, this was right, and damn hadn't they come so far since meeting?

Cooper squeezed his hand and Noah returned it, unable to hold back his grin at the sea of ugly sweaters at their wedding. Only his partner. Only the man who would soon be his husband would do something like this.

Cooper's aunt waited for them in front of the sliding glass door, so many emotions in her eyes. When they stopped in front of her, and the music quieted, Cooper whispered, "Thank you."

And she replied, "They would be the happiest parents in the world, today. Words can't express how proud of you they would be."

Jesus, but even Noah's heart skipped a few beats at that. He knew how important those words were to Cooper, and they were important to Noah as well. He wanted nothing more than to be a good man for Coop.

The rest of the ceremony went by in somewhat of a blur. He couldn't take his eyes off Cooper as Autumn spoke. His knees damn near went out when she asked Cooper to repeat after her. It was then that he remembered—"You know me better than that. I took care of the rings, too."

Cooper pulled a ring from his pocket and slipped it on Noah's finger. It was a simple band, white-gold, it looked like, with milgrain edges.

And then it was Noah's turn. Coop's eyes were wet as Noah spoke to him, as he promised to love him for eternity, and damn if Noah's eyes didn't sting as well.

Autumn handed him a ring that matched his own. He slid it down Cooper's finger, and his chest squeezed, his heart grew as though he didn't have space for it anymore.

This was his life. This man was his world, and he couldn't believe how lucky he was that Cooper chose to give himself to Noah.

And now they were husbands.

Noah pulled Cooper against him. Maybe he was supposed to go easy, but that wasn't his style. The guests were going to get a show because he wanted to kiss his husband senseless. Noah slipped his tongue in Coop's mouth, swallowed Cooper's moan. Fisted his hand in the damn ugly sweater, pulling Cooper as close to him as they could get.

He heard Braden mutter, "Damn," in the background and then Jessie say, "That's a bad word!"

He realized maybe he should stop there before they got *too* much of a show. He pulled back just as Braden replied to her, "It's not *that* bad."

He heard Wes's, "Shh!" before everyone started clapping. If Noah was being honest, he was ready for everyone to be gone so he could make love to his new husband.

-8-

THE CONGRATULATIONS NEVER seemed to end. Cooper was thankful for them all, glad that everyone had come out, but he hadn't thought this through very well. How long would everyone want to stay? Would they want to party the night away when all he wanted was to lock himself in his bedroom with Noah?

"You really had no idea about this?" Mason asked Noah as they stood off to the side of the room with Mason, Gavin, Braden and Wes.

"Not a fucking one. Well, I guess not unless you count the ten minute warning he gave me."

"Crazy bastard." Braden nudged Cooper. "Trying to show the rest of us up, huh?"

"I didn't really have to try, I'm just that good." They all laughed and Cooper realized how fucking lucky he was, how lucky they all were. Life didn't get much better than this.

It was another hour or so before the party started to clear out. He had Gavin and Mason to thank for that. Mason pulled him aside and mentioned that after proposing to Gavin last week, all he'd wanted was to get the hell out of there and fuck all night. He figured Cooper and Noah wanted the same, so the couple nonchalantly began steering people toward the door.

Cooper owed him one.

The couple stood at the door watching as the final lights disappeared down their driveway. The second Cooper closed the door, Noah shoved him against it.

Cooper's whole body burned with bone-deep desire as Noah

roughly grabbed his face and their mouths collided.

Frantically they ate at each other's mouths, their hands grabbed at each other's bodies, fingers dug into hip bones as they rubbed and kissed and tried to climb inside each other.

"I want you in our bed," Noah said when he pulled away. "But I want you down here, too. Under the lights."

Did he think this was going to be over quickly? "We have all night. We can make love in every room in the house. It'll be our husband fuck-fest," Cooper told him and Noah laughed. Coop kissed him as he did, and they laughed against each other's lips.

"I am so fucking in love with you, Cooper Bradshaw."

"I'm so fucking in love with you, Noah Bradshaw."

Noah swallowed, his adam's apple bobbed and he closed his eyes, let out a deep breath and smiled. "I want that sexy mouth of yours on me, but I want to suck you, too."

He pulled Cooper to the living room and Coop went easily. He'd follow Noah anywhere.

"All night," Cooper reminded him.

When they made it to the living room, Noah pushed Cooper down to the couch. The second he hit the cushions, Noah dropped to his knees.

His usually skilled fingers fumbled with the button and zipper on Cooper's pants, before he finally pulled them open. "Ass up." He swatted Cooper's leg and Coop leaned up. He took his pants and underwear off and then his mouth slid all the way down Cooper's aching erection.

"Oh fuck," Cooper groaned out, trying to keep himself from fucking Noah's mouth.

He shuddered, loving the feel of the wet suction of Noah's mouth.

"No, don't hold back, baby. This is meant to be quick and dirty. We'll go slow next time."

That was all Cooper needed to hear. He thrust his hips. Each time he did, Noah swallowed him down. He played with Cooper's balls as Cooper fucked his mouth.

Noah knew exactly how to work Cooper's cock. He knew how to deep-throat him, knew how to suck him and lick him just right. He pulled back, only keeping the crown of Cooper's dick in the heat of his mouth, his cheeks hollowing out with the gentle pulls of his lips.

"Fuck, Noah. You're going to make me come too fast." And he didn't want to, but like he said, this wasn't the end of it for tonight.

At that Noah took him deep again, Cooper pumping his hips. He grabbed Noah's hair in a tight grip. His balls got tighter and tighter as Noah palmed them. He wanted to hold his orgasm off, really he fucking wanted to, but he couldn't stop his balls from emptying, his seed pumping from his dick and into Noah's waiting mouth. Noah kept sucking, swallowing every last drop until Cooper was sure he'd never come again.

His bones melted. His body liquefied. Cooper sunk into the couch convinced he couldn't move. "I'm dead," he told Noah.

"You're beautiful." There was a catch in Noah's voice, which made Cooper open his eyes. He saw it, saw all that fucking love and emotion in Noah's dark brown eyes.

"I'm not the only one." Cooper winked at him, trying to lighten the mood. "We make a sexy couple."

"We do." Noah nodded, and then stood. The bulge behind the fly of his jeans was obvious. Cooper reached for him, ready to have Noah in his mouth, but his husband slapped his hand away. "No. Not yet. Let's go upstairs."

Noah held his hand out to Cooper, and Cooper took it. He pulled Coop up kissed his knuckles, and Cooper couldn't help but remember when he'd hurt his hand hitting the wall because he was so confused over his feelings for Noah. They'd come so damn far.

"Don't move." Noah ran a hand through Cooper's hair and then walked away, making a loop around the room blowing out all of the candles. He turned off the lights, grabbed Cooper's hand again and led him upstairs into their bathroom.

He started a shower and slipped out of his clothes. Cooper reached for his erection standing tall and proud, but Noah shook his head. "Not yet."

He pulled Cooper into the shower, where he washed every inch of his body before doing the same to himself. "Why don't I get to play?" Cooper asked.

"You will." Noah grinned. His erection was gone now. Cooper frowned at him, but Noah just continued his shower routine. Once they were done, he turned off the water and stepped out.

He gave Cooper a towel and then took one for himself. They dried off in silence, and then Noah was grabbing his hand and pulling him to their bedroom.

"There are not enough words in this world to describe how much I love you," Noah said as they stood at the foot of their bed.

Cooper's pulse sped up. He would never get tired of hearing that. "The same goes for you."

"It's time to take it slow, husband."

"I like the sound of that, husband."

Noah got onto their bed, lying on his back, his head against the pillows. Cooper made a home on top of him as he took Noah's mouth slowly and passionately. There was no rush as their tongues tangled together, just savoring each other's taste.

He loved the feel of Noah's hard body against his. The heat of him. The feel of his erection growing as they kissed and rubbed their dicks together. He could do this all fucking night—just kiss him.

Noah wrapped his arms around Cooper. Palmed his ass, making Cooper groan. Noah's finger traced the crack of his ass, and Cooper thrust against him harder, his whole body becoming more and more alive by the second.

He kissed Noah's neck, down his chest, licked his nipple piercings.

He didn't stop there, though. He kept kissing, kept licking

his way down Noah's taut body until he got to his now swollen prick. Cooper started at the crown, licking a path all the way down, before sucking Noah's heavy balls into his mouth. He smelled and tasted the soap on his skin. Loved the gentle pull of Noah's hand in his hair as he kept tonguing Noah's sac. All too soon Noah stopped him, tilting Cooper's head up so they were looking into each other's eyes.

"I want you to take me tonight, baby. I need to feel you inside of me."

Lust shot through Cooper. Noah was mostly a top and that suited them just fine. He loved being fucked by Noah...but he enjoyed doing the fucking from time to time, too. It wasn't often that Noah asked for it. He didn't know why, but it felt right tonight.

"Make love to me, Coop."

Cooper pressed a kiss to the head of Noah's prick, tasting the pre-come there. "Yeah...yeah, I want nothing more than to stake my claim on you tonight. You're officially mine now."

"I always have been."

Yes, he had.

-9-

NOAH NEEDED COOPER inside of him tonight. Needed to be full of nothing but Cooper.

His husband kneeled and grinned down at Noah. "Roll over," he said.

Noah did as told while Cooper reached over, grabbing the lube from their bedside table and dropping it to the bed.

He lay on his stomach now, legs wide as Cooper settled between them.

"Jesus, this ass." Cooper ran his hand around Noah's globes.

"Why don't you taste it?" Noah asked, thrusting against their bed and then pushing his ass out, closer to Cooper.

"I will. Slow now, remember. I'm gonna savor you."

"You can savor me every day."

"I will."

That's what he wanted to hear.

Cooper pressed a soft kiss to Noah's ass, licked his crack, and then started kissing again. Noah was burning up, his body aflame. His hole aching to be full and his cock begging to spill. "Coop."

"Noah."

Suddenly Cooper spread his cheeks wide and tongued his rim. Noah moaned as he lashed over the tender pucker. Quick tonguing, slow tonguing. He fucked the bed, needing friction. Each time he thrust, the bed rubbed his dick. Each time he stuck his ass out, Cooper's face was buried in it.

He tensed up when he felt Cooper's finger there, then relaxed as he probed him, pumping inside him before his tongue joined in. Both sensations making Noah call out, making goosebumps spread down his body.

Why had he said slow? He really wanted to fuck.

"Cooper…" he felt another wet finger at his hole, pushing in. Noah gripped the blanket, squeezed it in his hands. Fingers were good, but right now he wanted cock. Wanted Cooper to make love to him. "Please, baby."

"I'm getting there." Cooper's warm breath teased his sensitive skin. "It's not often I'm the one doing this. It's fun to get to tease and torture you the way you do me."

If that's how Cooper wanted to play this, wait until he saw what Noah had in store for their next round.

Cooper pushed his two fingers deep, rubbing Noah's prostate and he felt his hole start to clench. His muscles tightened as pleasure ricocheted around his body.

Cooper didn't stop, kept teasing him with his fingers and mouth until Noah thought he would lose his mind.

"Cooper…fuck, baby, please." He thrust against the bed again just as Cooper growled behind him.

"Christ, what it does to me to hear you beg."

And then his fingers were gone. He turned Noah over, pulling his legs open and up to his chest to give Cooper all the access he needed.

Cooper lubed his prick, then Noah's hole before leaning over him. The crown of his cock pressed against Noah's opening, and as soon as they kissed, he started to slowly work his way in.

Noah gritted his teeth as Cooper's thick erection pressed into him, filled him. It was an adjustment. It had been months since Cooper had him, but then suddenly…it wasn't enough. He needed to be stretched and filled and claimed the way Cooper said he wanted to claim him. Noah wrapped his arms around Coop, grabbing his ass and pulling him all the way inside.

They both called out, clutched at each other, Cooper buried deep in his ass.

"Give it to me, Coop. I'm yours. Your husband. Make love to me. Fuck me."

Cooper pulled almost all the way out and then slammed forward again. Each time he thrust, Noah savored the fullness. Each time he pulled back, Noah wanted him back.

It was a give and take, a tug-o-war. Fast then slow, as their mouths fused together, unhurriedly kissing and making love.

"You feel so good, Noah. So God damned good."

"You too, baby. I'm close. Christ, I'm close already."

Cooper pulled back far enough so Noah could stroke his cock. It pulsed in his hand, heat radiating through it. His balls felt the familiar burn and tingle. They hurt they were drawn so tight, ready to empty.

"I'm close too, fuck, Noah." He pulled out and then thrust again. Hard. Over and over he gave it to Noah with powerful pumps of his hips.

Noah couldn't hold back any longer. He erupted, letting go, come pulsing from his dick and down between his fingers as he kept working his own shaft.

"Oh, fuck." Cooper tensed over him, went nearly rigid, but still kept fucking through it. Noah felt the first jet fill him, and Cooper just kept thrusting, kept filling him up as he rode out his orgasm.

When he fell down on top of Noah, they didn't move, just held each other. They were a tangle of sweaty bodies with dried come between them.

"I love you, Noah," Cooper said after who knew how long.

"I love you too, Cooper."

They didn't untangle from each other most of the night. Only moving when one of them woke up horny and wanted to play, or needed to go to the bathroom. They stayed in their bed, naked, most of Christmas as well.

The town would feel deserted, practically empty, as people stayed inside with their loved ones celebrating the holiday. There was no one Noah wanted to be with other than Cooper.

"Do you want to get out of the house for a little while?" he asked Cooper. It was nearly three in the afternoon and they hadn't even eaten a real meal all day.

"Sure."

Noah didn't know where he wanted to go, just that he felt like being outside. Like he wanted the world to see his new husband even though it was unlikely they would run into anyone.

They took a quick shower and got dressed, bundling up because it was cold as hell outside. A few minutes later they were driving down Main Street in Coop's truck.

When Noah looked out the window, he noticed the park, the one with the tree. It was only lit at night, except on Christmas Day when they kept it on all day. "Pull over."

Cooper did and they both got out of the vehicle. They held hands and made their way to the oversized tree to admire it. It really was beautiful, though Noah was flying so high he would think that about anything right now.

"Come on." He tugged gently on Cooper's hand. They made their way to the small bridge that crossed the creek. Snow was all around them and it was cold as hell. They had no business being out here, but he was glad they were.

They stopped walking when they got to the middle of the bridge. Noah pulled his gloves off, rubbing Cooper's ring on his finger. He shoved his gloves into his pocket, grabbed Coop's hand, pulled his glove off and then looked at them together, their ringed fingers.

There wasn't a time in his life before Cooper that he ever thought he would get married. He'd never wanted it until this man. Maybe that's what love was: wanting things, no, *needing* things you'd never needed before. "I am so proud to be your husband."

"Even though we had an ugly sweater wedding?"

Noah smiled at him, his heart full. "*Because* we had an ugly sweater wedding."

This town, this man, they were the only two homes Noah had ever known, and he couldn't wait to continue living his life with his husband.

Epilogue

"CHELLE, SWEETHEART, YOU need to be still so Daddy can get you into your car seat. We're already running late." Braden tried again and failed to latch the belt. The toddler wanted nothing to do with the whole *being still* thing. She never did, and according to his mom, she was just like he'd been at her age.

Chelle wiggled and squirmed, reaching over for her brother who sat in his chair on the other side of the bench seat. Chase looked at her with serious, hazel eyes that were a mirror image of Wes's, and said, "No, Chelle." Of course Wes was able to easily strap their son into the seat while his twin giggled and gave Braden a hard time.

"Do you need my help?" Jessie asked Braden and he shook his head. She was great with the kids. She loved being a big sister. She helped him and Wes a lot, but Braden could also see the smile teasing her lips as she stood beside Wes, watching Braden try to handle the energetic girl.

Wes wore a matching near-grin on his face as well.

"Ha, ha. They think they're so funny, don't they, kiddo?" Braden tickled Chelle's stomach, and then managed to get the seat belt strapped. She was a handful, this one.

When Wes moved out of the way, Jessie climbed into the backseat of their SUV, sitting between the two car seats. Braden grabbed the suitcase from the ground and met Wes at the back. Once they had everything inside, Braden closed the door and Wes chuckled.

"She's just like you. It cracks me up to see the two of you butt heads."

"They say terrible twos, but I think it's more like the terrible threes." Not that Braden would change it for the world. He loved his life, and his family, but Chelle was definitely a little pistol.

"What's your excuse then? The terrible thirties?" Wes teased, and Braden shook his head.

Wes was right, though, Chelle looked more like his side of the family and had Braden's personality to the T. Chase, on the other hand, was all Wes. He was cautious, quieter, more willing to let his sister test the waters before he risked anything, and Chelle was always up for the risking.

"When'd you get so funny?" Braden pressed a quick kiss to Wes's lips. "I'll drive first."

"Oh, nice. You get to drive to Noah and Cooper's and then I get to drive to Mom and Dad's? That seems fair." Wes winked at him and Braden kissed him again. They were heading to Noah and Cooper's annual Christmas Eve party. From there they'd go spend a few days with Braden's family, the way they had for the past few years.

"Who gives a shit about fair? I'm quicker than you. That's all I need."

They smiled at each other and made their way into the vehicle.

"Ouch!" he heard Jessie say the second they got inside. "Chelle, stop pulling my hair!"

He could see Wes bite back a smile as he leaned toward the backseat. "Chelle, it's not nice to pull hair. Tell your sister you're sorry."

"Sowwy," Chelle said, mischief in her voice.

"Did you put the crayons and coloring books for Chase in the backseat?" Wes asked as they drove away.

"Yes, dear."

"What about Chelle's superhero action figure?"

"Yes, Wesley." Warmth spread through Braden's chest.

"We can always grab what we need after the party, but you

know Chelle will want her action figure and Chase will be calm the whole time in the car if he can color. Oh, did you grab the little travel table we got for him? I—"

"Color? Crayons?" Chase asked from the back, cutting Wes off.

"I got it," Jessie said, as Braden told Wes, "It's all in a bag at Jessie's feet. This isn't my first rodeo." He winked at Wes, who shook his head.

"There's nothing wrong with double checking."

"No, there's not." There was a lot more double checking of things in the beginning. The doctors spoke with them and they made the decision to fertilize more than one egg. Still, it had taken a little getting used to when they found out Lizzy was, in fact, carrying two babies.

Braden was excited. Wes a little nervous. Once the twins came, he borrowed some of Wes's nerves because holy hell two babies was hard, but then something strange happened…Wes, actually. Yeah, he was sometimes a little anal about things, but Braden realized how much that helped. Wes made a schedule and organized the new house in ways Braden never would have thought of. He'd been their savior.

He'd always known Wes would be a fantastic father, as he was with Jessie, but once the twins came, he'd excelled in ways Braden never would have imagined.

He'd taken a year off work to stay with the kids. He spent his days painting, and being the father he'd never had. Chase shared his love of art. Braden could watch the two of them sit at the table coloring for hours…when Chelle wasn't keeping him busy, running around like crazy, at least.

Wes only worked part time now. He was actually able to sell paintings every now and then. The extra money helped, and Wes got to do what he loved.

They were happy, so fucking happy that Braden couldn't help but count his blessings every day.

It didn't take them long to drive to Noah and Cooper's

house. The driveway was already full of cars when they pulled in.

"I hate being late," Wes said.

"We have three kids, Wesley. People expect us to be late."

They unloaded the twins, Wes carrying Chelle, and Braden holding Chase as they made their way across the snowy ground. They didn't have the chance to knock before Cooper pulled the door open for them. "Hey, man, Merry Christmas." Cooper hugged Braden and then held his hands out for Chase. "What's up, little man?"

Chase loved Cooper. He figured it would be Chelle who attached herself to him, but it wasn't. It was Chase. The two of them were buddies.

"Nuthin'," Chase answered him.

The house was full of people. Music played softly in the room as everyone laughed and talked. Wes set Chelle down just as Noah, Mason and Gavin walked over.

"Play?" Chelle asked Gavin. She loved music. She went crazy when Jessie had piano lessons, and he figured they'd have to start her pretty soon as well.

"I brought my guitar. We'll see what we can do." Gavin ruffled her brown hair. Chelle smiled at him and then ran off to make sure the world knew she was there.

"Where's Matthew?" Jessie asked Mason.

"He's in the living room. He's been waiting for you to get here," Mason replied.

Gavin and Mason had adopted Matthew the year before. It was a process they started right after getting married. They'd wanted an older child. Braden figured the couple wanted someone they thought needed them, and they'd found that person in Matthew. It had been rough in the beginning. He'd been in the system for a few years, had trouble in school and didn't believe the men would keep him, but he was now thriving with Gavin and Mason. Gavin took the time to help him in school in ways no one ever had and he'd just made the honor roll for the first time.

He was a funny kid, a little shy, but it was obvious he adored Mason and Gavin. They'd taken him hiking quite a bit this past summer, and from what Jessie told him, Matthew said it was one of his favorite things. Braden knew they had a trip planned this summer for the three of them. Matthew talked about it all the time.

He and Jessie had become the best of friends. Braden and Gavin both enjoyed watching them together, since they'd been friends so long themselves.

Braden watched as their oldest child walked away to find her friend. The kid was eleven going on thirty. She made them proud on a daily basis.

He grabbed Wes's hand and followed their friends into the house. Gavin's mom sat in one of the chairs. She rented a small house in Blackcreek now, so she could be close to Gavin. Cooper's aunt sat in the chair beside her, the two women talking to each other.

"So what's the plan this year? Have any surprises up your sleeve that we should all be aware of?" Wes asked Cooper.

The group of men made their way over to the corner of the room. Braden saw Chelle walk over and start to climb all over her sister and Matthew.

"Nope. No surprises this year. I already have everything I want." Cooper leaned back into Noah, who massaged his shoulders. Noah's business was flourishing. It had really picked up the past couple of years. They'd done some traveling, and more work on the house.

He knew fatherhood wasn't in their future. Different strokes and all. Both Noah and Coop doted on Matthew, Jessie, Chase and Chelle. Braden had asked him about it once because they were both so good with kids. Cooper had told him so many things in their lives had been out of their control—their families, losing people, being torn apart—and now that they had each other, they already had everything they needed. That was the perfect answer to Braden. It was exactly how he saw Noah and

Cooper. The men spoiled the kids close to them, but for them, they just held fast to each other.

"Who said we don't have a theme this year?" Noah asked, surprising him.

Braden, Wes, Gavin and Mason all looked at him.

"It's family—by blood or by choice, it doesn't matter." Noah touched Chase's hair as Cooper continued to hold him.

Wes reached over and grabbed Braden's hand. Gavin did the same to Mason. Braden's eyes locked on Jessie and Matthew, chatting across the room. He was looking at her nail polish as Jessie animatedly spoke to him about it.

And yeah, the theme made sense. They were all family: Noah, Cooper, Gavin, Mason, Matthew, Braden, Wes, Jessie, Chase and Chelle.

They were all damn lucky.

"I wanted to go with The Incredible World of Noah and Cooper, but Noah wouldn't let me," Coop said and they all laughed.

They'd had their share of ups and downs, hard times and blessings. They knew life was messy and imperfect—they would disagree and drive each other crazy, but in the end, it was their love that bound all of them together.

Things couldn't get and better than this, than these people and the life they shared in Blackcreek.

And they all lived happily ever after...

Find Riley:

Newsletter

Reader's Group
facebook.com/groups/RileysRebels2.0

Facebook
facebook.com/rileyhartwrites

Twitter
twitter.com/RileyHart5

Goodreads
goodreads.com/author/show/7013384.Riley_Hart

Instagram
instagram.com/rileyhartwrites

BookBub
bookbub.com/profile/riley-hart

Acknowledgment

A special thanks goes to Jessica de Ruiter and Hope Cousin. You seriously save me on a daily basis, whether helping with the group, letting me bounce ideas off of you, reading for me, or just letting me vent. I probably wouldn't have written this book without you guys. Our chats were so helpful and I can't thank you enough for all that you do.

I'd also like to thank Mirjana for your incredible insight and sharp eye. Keyanna for proofreading, and thanks to Wendy and Kim for your eye as well.

I have to thank Riley's Rebels. I love our group and each one of you. You make my days brighter.

As always, thank you to my readers. I love this journey we're on together.

Other Books by Riley Hart

Series by Riley Hart
Inevitable
Secrets Kept
Briar County
Atlanta Lightning
Blackcreek
Boys In Makeup with Christina Lee
Broken Pieces
Crossroads
Fever Falls with Devon McCormack
Finding
Forbidden Love with Christina Lee
Havenwood
Jared and Kieran
Last Chance
Metropolis with Devon McCormack
Rock Solid Construction
Saint and Lucky
Stumbling Into Love
Wild side

Standalone books:
Boyfriend Goals
Strings Attached
Beautiful & Terrible Things
Love Always
Endless Stretch Of Blue
Looking For Trouble
His Truth

Standalone books with Devon McCormack:
No Good Mitchell
Beautiful Chaos
Weight Of The World
Up For The Challenge

Standalone books with Christina Lee:
Science & Jockstraps
Of Sunlight and Stardust

About the Author

Riley Hart's love of all things romance shines brightly in everything she writes. Her primary focus is Male/Male romance but under various pen names, her prose has touched practically every part of the spectrum of love and relationships. The common theme that ties them all together is stories told from the heart.

A hopeless romantic herself, Riley is a lover of character-driven plots, many with flawed and relatable characters. She strives to create stories that readers can not only fall in love with, but also see themselves in. Real characters and real love blended together equal the ultimate Riley Hart experience.

When Riley isn't creating her next story, you can find her reading, traveling, or dreaming about reading or traveling, and spending time with her two perfectly snarky kids, and one swoon-inducing husband.

Riley Hart is represented by Jane Dystel at Dystel, Goderich & Bourret Literary Management. She's a 2019 Lambda Literary Award Finalist for *Of Sunlight and Stardust.*

Made in the USA
Middletown, DE
17 March 2023

26989271R00086